This month, in

THE BACHELOR TAKES A WIFE
by Jackie Merritt

Meet Keith Owens—the most eligible
millionaire in Royal, Texas. He's a businessman
who always gets what he wants, and what he
wants now is Andrea O'Rourke, his high school
sweetheart. Keith will do just about anything
to reignite the passion he and Andrea once
shared—but will he stick around when he
discovers Andrea's little secret?

SILHOUETTE DESIRE
IS PROUD TO PRESENT THE

TEXAS Cattleman's Club
The Last Bachelor

**Five wealthy Texas bachelors—all members of
the state's most exclusive club—set out to
uncover the traitor in their midst...
and find true love.**

Dear Reader,

Summer vacation is simply a state of mind...so create your dream getaway by reading six new love stories from Silhouette Desire!

Begin your romantic holiday with *A Cowboy's Pursuit* by Anne McAllister. This MAN OF THE MONTH title is the author's 50th book and part of her CODE OF THE WEST miniseries. Then learn how a Connelly bachelor mixes business with pleasure in *And the Winner Gets...Married!* by Metsy Hingle, the sixth installment of our exciting DYNASTIES: THE CONNELLYS continuity series.

An unlikely couple swaps insults and passion in Maureen Child's *The Marine & the Debutante*—the latest of her popular BACHELOR BATTALION books. And a night of passion ignites old flames in *The Bachelor Takes a Wife* by Jackie Merritt, the final offering in TEXAS CATTLEMAN'S CLUB: THE LAST BACHELOR continuity series.

In *Single Father Seeks...* by Amy J. Fetzer, a businessman and his baby captivate a CIA agent working under cover as their nanny. And in Linda Conrad's *The Cowboy's Baby Surprise,* an amnesiac FBI agent finds an undreamed-of happily-ever-after when he's reunited with his former partner and lover.

Read these passionate, powerful and provocative new Silhouette Desire romances and enjoy a sensuous summer vacation!

Joan Marlow Golan

Joan Marlow Golan
Senior Editor, Silhouette Desire

Please address questions and book requests to:
Silhouette Reader Service
U.S.: 3010 Walden Ave., P.O. Box 1325, Buffalo, NY 14269
Canadian: P.O. Box 609, Fort Erie, Ont. L2A 5X3

The Bachelor
Takes a Wife
JACKIE MERRITT

Published by Silhouette Books

America's Publisher of Contemporary Romance

Special thanks and acknowledgment are given to Jackie Merritt for her contribution to the TEXAS CATTLEMAN'S CLUB: THE LAST BACHELOR series.

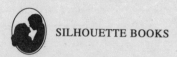 SILHOUETTE BOOKS

ISBN 0-373-76444-8

THE BACHELOR TAKES A WIFE

Visit Silhouette at www.eHarlequin.com

Printed in U.S.A.

JACKIE MERRITT

is still writing, just not with the speed and constancy of years past. She and hubby are living in southern Nevada again, falling back on old habits of loving the long, warm or slightly cool winters and trying almost desperately to head north for the months of July and August, when the fiery sun bakes people and cacti alike.

"What's Happening in Royal?"

NEWS FLASH, June—As usual, Royal's Texas Cattleman's Club ball was a smashing success! Could there have been any doubt? Glamorous women, sexy gents, fabulous food...and all for a wonderful cause. This year's charity is Royal's very own New Hope battered women's shelter. New Hope's representative, Andrea O'Rourke, was on hand at the ball to receive the hefty donation, along with the exclusive attentions of millionaire Keith Owens....

Ms. O'Rourke has refused to discuss her relationship to the debonair tycoon, but sources tell us that Andrea and Keith were a hot item back in their high school days.... Is there still something simmering between them? If so, the ladies of Royal are going to have to look elsewhere for an eligible man. This elusive executive may be going down for the count.

Do the members of the Texas Cattleman's Club know who murdered Eric Chambers? Rumor has it that the culprit may be a club member.... Is there a traitor among them? If so, the murderer had better watch out, because justice is closing in....

Prologue

Keith Owens was well aware of Jason Windover's air of contentment as he and his friends prepared cups of coffee for themselves at a serving cart, then sat in comfortable chairs around a table in one of the Cattleman's Club's private meeting rooms. Jason good-naturedly laughed off the teasing remarks about his and Merry's honeymoon, from which they'd returned only the day before, because it was all in fun and he'd expected some tongue-in-cheek banter from his buddies. But he wasn't above giving back at least part of what he was getting, and Keith, being the only bachelor remaining in the group, just naturally seemed to be his best target.

"Just you wait, old pal," Jason drawled. "Some sweet-lookin' little gal is out there this very minute, just biding her time for the right moment to rope and hog-tie Royal's most elusive executive."

"Elusive executive?" Keith repeated with a laugh, and looked around the table for confirmation or denial from Sebastian Wescott, William Bradford, Robert Cole and, of course, Jason, all of whom wore big smiles. "Is that what I am?"

"Sounds like an apt description to me," Sebastian said. "Good work, Jason."

"Thanks," Jason said with a cocky grin at Keith.

"All right, I get it," Keith said. "I'm the last bachelor among you jokers, and you're not going to let me forget it. Well, put this in your pipes and smoke it, old friends. I happen to enjoy bachelorhood."

"So did we when we were young and foolish," Rob said with an overly dramatic sigh.

Everyone laughed, because they'd *all* been bachelors only five months ago and they'd been neither young nor foolish. Only one thing had happened to change their status from single to married—falling in love, which was a mighty powerful force, as they had discovered. And not a man around that table—other than Keith—believed that Royal's "elusive executive" would remain a bachelor for long. After all, hadn't he already tossed his hat in the ring by naming New Hope Charity for battered women as the beneficiary of the Cattleman's Club's annual charity benefit? That decision would bring Andrea O'Rourke, Keith's old college flame, back into his life, since she was the volunteer at New Hope who dealt firsthand with public donations. It seemed to the men around the table that if Keith hadn't wanted contact with Andrea, then he would have named an entirely different charity to receive this year's check.

No one said so, though, as some subjects weren't up for open and verbal conjecture. They could tease Jason, because he'd just come back from his honeymoon, but they couldn't make light of Keith's sudden interest in renewing ties with Andrea.

"Much as I'm enjoying this," Keith interjected, "I think it's time we got down to the reason we called this meeting. Dorian." The other four friends sobered at once. They all shared the strong suspicion that Dorian Brady had murdered

Eric Chambers, an accountant at Wescott Oil. But so far, they had no proof of his involvement.

Keith continued. "We've been doing our best to keep an eye on Dorian during your absence, Jason, and none of us have spotted anything suspicious. In fact, it appears that, if anything, Dorian has been deliberately maintaining a low profile."

"That's suspicious in itself," Jason said. "Don't you agree, Sebastian?"

"Dorian was never low-key before," Sebastian soberly agreed. He was understandably more deeply affected by recent events than the others, since Dorian was his half brother. "Except when it fitted his agenda. As you all know, his showing up out of the blue was one hell of a shock. We look so much alike, I never for a minute doubted his story about Dad being his father, and I still don't. Putting him to work at Wescott Oil was a bad error in judgment, however. My only excuse was that I really wanted to help him."

"None of what happened is your fault, Sebastian," Keith said quietly. "How do honest people deal with a snake like Dorian? He's deliberately gone out of his way to undermine your authority and good reputation with the company and the community in general. Don't blame yourself for anything Dorian's done."

"Considering his background with Merry's sister even before he came to Royal, he was a louse then and he's a louse now," Jason said stonily. No one could disagree with that summation, and the conversation changed directions.

"What we still can't figure out is his motive for murder. What was Eric Chambers to him, other than a co-worker? It simply doesn't add up."

"And let's not forget Dorian's alibi," Will said. "Maybe we should talk to Laura Edwards about that. Double-check her story about Dorian being at the diner at the time of Eric's murder."

"Why would she lie?" Sebastian asked and got up for a coffee refill. "I've wrestled with motive since the murder, and I have a hunch that it's somehow connected to me. Jason, I know you were uneasy about Dorian from the start." Sebastian resumed his seat. "Why?"

"We've covered this ground before," Keith said.

"Yes, but obviously we're missing something," Sebastian said. He frowned slightly and added, "What could it be?"

"His computer files imply that Dorian was blackmailing Eric," Jason reminded them all. "Merry discovered that."

"Yes, but those files do not explain the blackmail. What was Eric up to that Dorian was able to discover and use against him? Maybe if we knew more about Eric," he mused. "What do we really know about him?"

"He worked for Wescott for quite a few years," Sebastian volunteered. "He was a very private individual with a cat as his only companion. He was divorced long before coming to work for Wescott, so no one I know has ever met his ex. He lived alone—with his cat—in a small house. That struck me as odd, because he made a good annual salary."

"Which he could have been paying to his ex-wife in alimony," Keith said.

"But he wasn't. His wife had remarried quite a while back, ending the alimony payments, and there were no children for Eric to support. He could've afforded a much better home, considering his earning power."

"Follow the money," Jason said, half in jest.

But the simple concept simultaneously struck all five men as critically important. They looked at each other, and several of them nodded. Months ago, money had gone missing at Wescott Oil. Sebastian, accused of killing Eric and taking the money—a ridiculous charge when he owned the company and had more money than he could ever spend—had been completely exonerated and all charges against him had been dropped. Since then, everyone had been concentrating on Eric's murder. The missing money was still unexplained, a loose end left dangling.

It could be the clue they had been hoping to uncover and follow up on.

One

Andrea O'Rourke was given the good news on the first of June. "New Hope has been named by the Texas Cattleman's Club as the primary beneficiary of this year's charitable donation!" The other volunteers present at the time were overjoyed and began discussing what could be done with the money. New Hope's most crucial need was money for expansion, but how much would the donation be? Everyone knew the club's annual charity ball donations were legendary, but the sums distributed to needy causes were never publicized.

Andrea tried to appear as thankfully elated as the other volunteers in the meeting room of the big old house that served as a sanctuary for battered and abused women. The building was the heart and soul of New Hope Charity, and the meeting room was pleasant with comfortable mismatched chairs, several desks where paperwork was taken care of, and a table with the tools and supplies to brew coffee and tea.

While Andrea rejoiced at New Hope's good fortune in her

own quiet, subdued way, she also suffered an internal ache that she would never even attempt to explain to these good ladies. Residents of Royal, Texas, knew that she was the volunteer who acted as New Hope's representative for events that benefited the charity. The more Andrea thought about it, the more suspicious she became that Keith Owens, longtime member of the Cattleman's Club and the one citizen of Royal whom Andrea tried diligently to avoid, was behind the good deed that had the other ladies in the room giddy with delight.

I'll have to attend the club's annual charity ball! I'll have to accept the donation with thanks, probably even have to say a few words about New Hope. Well, I've done that before at other events, but not with Keith Owens looking on and undoubtedly smiling that overbearing, egotistical smile of his while I'm on stage!

Oh, my heavens! What if he's the member passing out the award?

No! I won't do it, I can't do it.

But of course she could do it, and she would, however painful to herself. Looking around at the generous women who gave time, energy, intelligence and individual talents to New Hope, Andrea was aware that none of them really knew her. They thought they did, and she encouraged that impression because her privacy was crucial to the quiet lifestyle she had fashioned for herself. She had lived alone since the death of her husband five years before, and her preference for dignity and serenity in everything from her home to her personal demeanor eliminated a good many people who had attempted a close friendship. Those friends who had made the cut were truly cherished by Andrea, and for the most part they enjoyed the same gentle entertainment that she did—primarily small dinner parties and elegant little luncheons at which intellectual discussions of literature, music, fashion and personal hobbies took place.

Keith Owens was not in that circle and never would be. Andrea had never stepped foot inside the Texas Cattleman's Club's sprawling two-and-a-half-story clubhouse—decorated, she'd heard, in dark paneling, heavy leather furniture and stuffed animal heads. Visualizing herself doing so the night of the charity ball actually made her shudder. She couldn't share that thought with the group, of course, and why would she? Were the intimate details of her life—past or present—anyone's business, but her own? Of course not.

Again scanning the women, Andrea uneasily wondered how many of them, if any, knew about her and Keith's commingled past. It seemed a silly concern when their history had ended almost twenty years ago—both she and Keith were thirty-eight years old now—but some people had such damnably long memories.

Andrea suddenly couldn't sit still a moment longer. Rising from her chair, she smiled at the group and said, "I'm terribly sorry, but I just remembered a very important appointment. I really must run."

The women accepted her story and bid her goodbye, and before Andrea had even gone through the door they were back to fantasizing about New Hope's windfall.

Andrea left with acidic resentment gnawing at her vitals. If it weren't for Keith Owens's participation in the club's gift to New Hope, she would have been as genuinely overjoyed as the other volunteers were.

Damn him! How dare he create disturbances on the smooth pathway of her daily existence after so many years?

Keith kept himself in good physical shape in his home gym. A personal trainer came to the house twice a week to put Keith through the paces, check his vitals and advise him on diet and general fitness. The rest of the week Keith worked out on his own. He liked exercising himself into a sweat, and his exertion, followed by a shower, always seemed to clear his head.

The morning after New Hope had been notified of the club's choice—most definitely an honor for any charity organization—Keith went to his gym with his usual good intentions. But he hadn't slept as well as he usually did, and instead of diving into his exercise program, he dawdled around for about ten minutes, then lost interest and went down to his kitchen for some coffee and the morning paper.

The coffee tasted good but he couldn't concentrate on the daily news. Frowning slightly he leaned back in his chair and stared off into space. He felt adrift, uncentered, and he didn't have to wonder why: It was all about anticipation and the knowledge that Andrea would be at the ball.

For years they had ignored each other, or *tried* to ignore each other. When something unforeseen and unpreventable brought them together—always briefly—they said hello, but Andrea's polite voice and unsmiling countenance emitted enough ice to chill to the bone anyone within hearing range. He had to ask himself why he was forcing them to meet again when Andrea had only tried to avoid him. He didn't doubt that she would be civil at the ball—he'd observed those cool, impeccable manners of hers more than once—but since when had an evening of distant, chilly civility from a woman held any appeal for him?

Deep down, Keith knew the answer to all of his questions about Andrea. He wanted things to be different between them. He wanted her to talk to him without that famous chill, to look at him and really see him, and to treat him as she once had. Would the ball change anything? Maybe not. *Probably* not, if he was completely honest about it. But it *was* an opportunity to spend some time with her.

Accepting that summation with a knot in his gut, Keith turned his thoughts to the problem of proving Dorian Brady's guilt. It was frustrating as hell to be certain of something and not be able to come up with enough evidence to take to the police. Mulling it over for at least the tenth time since his last meeting with Sebastian, Rob, Jason and Will, something that had been niggling at Keith abruptly rose to the surface. Getting up from the table, he went to the telephone, took it from its cradle and walked around the room while he dialed a number.

"Sebastian? I'm glad I caught you. Listen, I'd like to pick

up Eric's computer. I should've thought of it before. I know the police checked the computer and so did Rob. He found Eric's personal journal and that e-mail message and, believe me, I'm not minimizing Rob's…or the police expert's… computer abilities, but if there's one thing I know through and through, it's computers. There could be more information in disguised or hidden files that everyone thus far has missed. I think I should check it out.''

Keith's extremely successful career had been built around computer software, and no one got very far with software unless they understood computer *hard*ware—the nuts and bolts of the machine, so to speak. He could take a computer apart and put it back together in mere minutes. Hell, he could build one from scratch if he had the components on hand. In some cases he could actually *create* the components. Owens Techware was a well-known and highly respected contributor of technical software the world over.

''Yes, you're the logical person to do that,'' Sebastian agreed with a spark of excitement in his voice. ''You may be on to something, Keith. Pick it up anytime. I had it put in storage.''

''Great. I'll come by Wescott Oil sometime today.''

After hanging up the phone, Keith let Andrea enter his mind again, but only for a few moments. Heaving a sigh because he had never understood himself where Andrea was concerned, he went to take the shower he should have taken earlier.

The elegant old clubhouse and its immaculate grounds seemed magical on ball night. Hundreds of tiny white lights bedecked shrubbery and trees, and every window in the building glowed with warm, golden light.

The limousine in which Andrea was riding crept toward the club's entrance. It was following a long line of luxury cars and limousines that stopped only long enough to dispatch beautifully dressed guests, so it was stop and go, stop and go, for about ten minutes.

Seated in the limousine's back seat Andrea drew a long breath rife with disapproval and dissatisfaction. She had accepted being manipulated into attending this year's ball, but she was adamant about it not happening again under any circumstances. If club members chose to bestow some of their wealth on New Hope again, she was going to weasel out of this duty by hook or by crook. She absolutely hated the club's insistence on picking her up in a showy limousine. She was not a limousine person, and she felt completely out of place in it.

This, too, she blamed on Keith Owens. No one would ever convince her that he hadn't dreamed up this whole scenario just to embarrass her, and, however much she would like to cut him cold tonight, she was going to have to smile and chat and act as though she didn't resent the air he breathed.

She had not willingly given Keith the time of day since college, though they ran into each other every so often. Accidental meetings—inevitable in towns the size of Royal, Texas—never failed to unnerve her. Just the sight of Keith raised her blood pressure and made the fine hairs on the back of her neck stand up, a condition she attributed to a mix of extreme tension and dislike. He had, after all, nearly destroyed her that night so long ago. That night when she'd naively expected a marriage proposal, and instead Keith had proposed a business partnership. A business partnership! He'd been full of himself then, and from the little she'd seen of him over the years, he was *still* full of himself.

On that particular night she'd been totally crushed and had angrily let him have it, making it clear that she was going to major in education and wanted nothing to do with his business plans. To make matters worse, Keith had derided *her* choice of careers—teaching—and boasted about *his* ambitions. Although Keith had made a fortune in computer software, Andrea had felt in her heart that her career rewards as a teacher far exceeded Keith's. But he would never, ever understand putting joy in one's personal accomplishments ahead of an ever-increasing bank account.

Andrea shook her head just as the limousine braked precisely at the club's main entrance. She disliked these particular trips down memory lane. Usually she had no trouble avoiding these memories in favor of those that gave her pleasure instead of riling emotions that she would rather not poke and prod to life.

The limo door was opened by a uniformed greeter. Andrea took his outstretched hand and allowed him to assist her from the vehicle. People were everywhere, she saw—going into the club or standing outside to chat. Laughter and conversation mingled with the muted music inside the club and floated out on the evening air. The dress code for the ball was formal, which had once dictated that men wore black. Not these days. There were tuxedoes in many different colors, and the males in attendance were almost as flamboyantly clad as their female companions. The ladies, however, were also gleaming from the exquisite jewelry around their necks, in their hair, on their wrists and fingers, and anywhere else they could attach diamonds, emeralds, pearls and rubies to their person.

The limousine moved away and another vehicle immediately took its place. Andrea began walking toward the entrance and gasped in surprise when someone took her arm.

"Good evening," Keith said, his lips brazenly close to her ear. "I wasn't sure whether you would arrive alone or with an escort, so I've been out here watching for you. Since you're alone, I'm appointing myself your guide, counselor, escort and buddy for this evening's festivities."

Despite her annoyance, Andrea couldn't help but register his good looks, which shook her aplomb and irritated her no end. His tuxedo was a wonderful shade of tan that was almost exactly the color of his light-caramel-hued hair. The quirky smile that had captured her heart back in college was still his best feature, although his thickly lashed dark-brown eyes ran a very close second. Admiring and eventually drooling over Keith Owens's good looks had caused her pain and heartache in her college years. Maturity had provided her with some advantages, thank goodness, one of which was an understanding of just how unimportant good looks really were. She'd figured that out only a few years after college, because the man she'd married had been wonderfully pleasant-looking but not drop-dead handsome, as Keith was. Frankly, everything about Keith galled her, especially his overbearing assumption that he could appoint himself her escort for the evening.

"I think not," she said coolly, trying to pull her arm out of his.

"Think again. It's only good protocol for our guest of honor to have an escort," Keith said smoothly while giving her a head-to-foot inspection. She was utterly beautiful. In college she'd been pretty, with long black hair and dark-blue eyes. Hell, she'd been cute as a button when she'd been a kid, a fact he remembered very well because they'd grown up next door to each other. But *cute* and *pretty* simply weren't the right words to describe how she looked now. Her figure was incredible, especially provocative in that two-piece ivory gown she was wearing. It fit like a dream, from its high neckline all the way down its classic lines to a hem incorporating one sexy slit that permitted brief glimpses of the lower portion of her left leg. It was a marvelous dress, Keith decided, its delightful color accenting Andrea's hair and eyes. Her black hair was much shorter now, but its simple style was extremely becoming to her beautiful face.

"If I had wanted or believed I needed an escort, I would have invited a friend to accompany me this evening. Your protocol is about fifty years outdated. You may find this a major shock to your good-old-country-boy beliefs, but nowadays women actually walk and talk all on their own. Please let go of my arm."

"I'll let go of yours if you'll take mine."

"How about if I kick you in the knee, put you out of commission and get rid of you that way?"

"Resorting to violence already, are we?"

Andrea shook off his hand with one big jerk of her arm.

"That's enough childish horseplay!" She started walking toward the entrance, fully aware of Keith keeping up with her every step. He wasn't going away, however rude she might be. She heaved a sigh. The evening was going to be as unbearable as she'd anticipated.

Inside the club there was a receiving line, and while Keith bantered and laughed with his friends greeting the arriving guests, Andrea smiled congenially, and furtively checked out the décor. It was as dreadfully macho as she'd been told. Was that a boar's head over the mantel? She shook hands and made appropriate comments to people she recognized but just barely knew. *Her* friends were not members of this club, which admittedly did a lot of good for the community but was also known for some very rowdy escapades. Now that Andrea was inside she could tell that the band was playing some very lively songs, mostly with a country-and-western slant. *Well, what did you expect? Schubert? Beethoven? Chopin?*

"My dear, we're all so proud of this year's choice of charities," an older woman, Janice Morrison, wife to a lifetime member of the club, said while gripping Andrea's hand in a long handshake. Mrs. Morrison's diamond necklace alone would have financed the operation of New Hope for five years, Andrea thought, although she certainly did not begrudge the congenial woman her astounding necklace. Andrea was wearing very little jewelry herself—a pearl-and-diamond ring and matching earrings—but she had some very good pieces in her safe. They were gifts from Jerry, her deceased husband, which was the only reason she kept them, because she hadn't worn the items since his death.

"We at New Hope are both proud and delighted," Andrea murmured. "Be assured that all donations will be put to very good use."

"I'm sure they will. My, you two make a fine-looking couple," Mrs. Morrison gushed.

The woman was gazing from her to Keith, and Andrea's smile faded a little as she withdrew her hand. Keith saved the day by quipping, "We're just a couple of old friends, Janice."

Janice Morrison wasn't convinced. "Who do you think you're kidding, Keith Owens?"

Andrea wilted internally. Here was a lady with a long memory, and there were probably dozens of others attending the ball that also remembered when the Vances and the Owenses—her parents and Keith's—had lived next door to each other. This time, when Keith took Andrea's arm to steer her away from the receiving line, she felt too weak to protest. How in heaven's name was she going to make it through an entire evening of innuendo and reminders and still keep on smiling?

"Sorry about that," Keith said to her.

Andrea forgot about smiling and her eyes flashed angrily. "Why would you expect anything else when you're sticking to me like glue?"

"Would you really rather be left on your own in this crowd?"

"I'd *rather* not give anyone the wrong impression!" Andrea glanced around. "Do you have any idea of how many people are looking at us right now?"

Keith glanced around himself, then grinned wickedly. "Quite a few, by the looks of it. Wonder what they're whispering about. Maybe they're wondering if we're sleeping together."

Andrea gaped at him. "Are you mad? We didn't even sleep together when we dated!"

"That sure wasn't my fault."

"Of course it wasn't. Since you had—and probably still do have—the morals of an alley cat."

"Don't tell me the subject of sex still embarrasses you. Andrea, you're a big girl now. Actually, when I think about it, you were a big girl in college, but you had far too many hang-ups for a..." Keith wisely closed his mouth. He'd been about to say something about randy young college men, but decided to avoid that topic for the present. "How about a glass of champagne?" he asked instead.

"If I say no are you going to go off and find someone else to badger?"

"Nope."

"Then yes, I'd like a glass of champagne."

"Great." Placing his hand on the small of her back, and enjoying a delicious tingle in his lower regions from the physical contact, Keith steered her through the crowd to one of the bars and ordered two glasses of champagne. After handing one to Andrea he smiled and said, "Cheers, sweetheart, and let me add that you've got what it takes."

Andrea felt heat rising in her cheeks and knew that she'd turned pink. "What on earth are you talking about? Why didn't you stop at 'cheers' and make this a tolerable occasion?"

"You know, I should have. Sometimes I say things without thinking. I mean, that was obviously a compliment, but if I had thought about it before speaking, I would probably have postponed it until you'd had a couple of glasses of champagne."

Andrea glared at him. "Meaning I would appreciate crude remarks then? You didn't know me in college and you don't know me now. I *never* liked your crudity, which you would remember for yourself if your self-serving, smug, conceited head wasn't bigger than Rhode Island!"

Keith roared with laughter. "Andy, I absolutely adore you."

"Oh, give me a break," she drawled, although her heart was suddenly pounding unmercifully fast. He didn't mean what he'd said, for heaven's sake. He was just the kind of man who said outrageous things to women and then laughed at their reactions. He obviously believed he was God's gift to womankind, and maybe he was—for some women—but he was no gift in her estimation. He was a cad without a conscience, and he didn't even have the grace to pretend otherwise.

He peered, owl-like, at her over the rim of his glass as he took another swallow. "How about a game of tit for tat?"

"Which is?" she asked, frowning and suspicious.

"I'll give you a break if you get rid of that stick up your spine. You used to be a fun person to be with. You used to laugh a lot. You're arguably the most beautiful woman here and if people are staring and speculating, that's why. After all, I've been single and alone for four years. I'd have to be crazy to be talking with the loveliest lady here and not let you—and everyone else—know that I'm interested."

Andrea gasped. "Do you actually have the temerity to think I *care* if you're interested?" Fury set in then, and she felt herself start to tremble. She had to get away from him before she let the whole crowd know that she could happily murder Keith Owens where he stood. "Which way is the ladies' room?" she asked. It was at that moment that she realized she didn't have her handbag. "Oh, no, I left it in the limousine!"

"Left what in the limo?"

"My handbag." She glared into Keith's eyes. If she hadn't been so unnerved by the evening ahead at the time of arrival, she never would have left anything in that accursed limousine. This, too, was Keith's fault. "Where do they park the limousines? I need to get my bag."

"I'll show you."

Just then a man's voice intruded on them. "Well, this must be the guest of honor, Andrea O'Rourke."

Both Andrea and Keith turned a bit to see the man. Keith's expression was no longer flirtatious and friendly, Andrea saw with some surprise. In fact, he was actually glowering at a very attractive man in an elegantly tailored black tuxedo.

"Aren't you going to introduce me, Keith?" the man asked in a dangerously slick voice. Andrea could tell that Keith didn't want this stranger even saying hello to her.

The man gave a dry little laugh. "Apparently the cat has taken hold of Keith's tongue. Permit me to introduce myself, Andrea. I'm Dorian Brady." He reached out and took An-

drea's hand. "This is an honor and a great pleasure," Dorian
said.

Andrea was not pleased. Dorian might be physically attractive, but something about him made her uneasy. She
pulled her hand from his and said, "Thank you." Keith was
still scowling at Dorian, which was puzzling, since Keith
seemed to be on friendly terms with all the other club members. "The directions to the parking lot, please?" Andrea
asked him stiffly.

"Well, I can see that the two of you are quite involved.
You will excuse me, won't you? Good evening, Andrea. Perhaps we will meet again." Dorian bowed slightly and departed.

"That creep," Keith mumbled. "Andrea, give that guy a
very wide berth."

"I plan to, but not because of *your* orders," she replied
sharply. "Now how do I find the limousine parking area?"

Keith pulled himself together. Dorian's unexpected intrusion had unnerved him. Actually, Keith had expected that
Dorian would avoid the ball, especially since Merry and Jason were there. Maybe it was time the club members voted
to revoke Dorian's membership. Keith couldn't remember a
member ever being banned before, but there must be something in the bylaws about membership reversal.

Calmer again, he said to Andrea, "Why don't I go and get
your handbag? I could do it in half the time it would take
you."

"Just give me the directions," she repeated.

"Fine," Keith said with a disgusted shake of his head. He
glanced around and was relieved to see nothing of Dorian.
He didn't want Andrea wandering the grounds alone with
Dorian hot on her trail. Maybe Dorian had shown his face
just to prove he could and had already left. "Go through that
far door, which leads to a patio restaurant, then leave the
patio and follow the main path through the flower garden, go
past the pool and you will reach the club's valet-parking area.

The limousines are usually parked on the right side of the lot.''

It sounded like a long walk to Andrea, and his offer to run and get her handbag made a lot more sense than her strolling that far on high heels. But she'd already refused his help, and pride wouldn't permit her to backtrack. Andrea handed him her glass. Then, with a stony expression and a clipped and unfriendly ''Thank you,'' she turned on her heel and headed for the far door.

Walking as fast as possible in her dressy high heels, Andrea easily followed Keith's directions. Her thoughts were still in a whirl from having to deal with Keith tonight. His mix of good looks, cocky personality and overwhelming self-confidence shouldn't be allowed. She'd fallen head over heels for him years before she should even have noticed that he was a boy and she a girl, and while it nearly killed her to admit such a thing tonight, he was still a dangerous distraction to her emotional well-being.

Did he affect every female that way, or was she particularly susceptible to him?

Impossible, she decided. He probably drew women the way honey drew bees. She was just feeling overheated because of a very old romance and she resented it so much that she had to blink back tears of frustration.

Keith had said she was fun in college, and that she had laughed a lot. Obviously he'd never seen beneath the laughter to the serious young woman underneath who had adored him since childhood. Much of it had been hero worship. He'd been her favorite playmate and the friend to whom she could tell anything. He'd been the first boy to kiss her. They'd been around eleven at the time and had decided that kissing wasn't nearly as much fun as swinging a bat in a softball game or doing cannonball leaps into a swimming pool.

High school had changed both of them. He'd become one of the swaggering superstar jocks, too cute to be believed and the target of every girl in school. Andrea had still adored him, but Keith's head had swelled intolerably from his sudden popularity and she hadn't been able to resist telling him to get real and to come back down to earth. He hadn't taken criticism well, and their friendship had cooled drastically so that they rarely had even said hello to one another. The summer after high-school graduation they'd gotten back together and were thrilled to learn they had both been accepted at the same college, their plan for many years before Keith had grown too big for his britches.

Oh, yes, she'd been fun and had laughed at everything. What girl wouldn't laugh a lot when she was in a wonderful college and had the best-looking, most popular boyfriend of any of her sorority sisters?

But then, of course, Keith began wanting more than kisses. And to be perfectly fair, she had wanted more than kisses, too. She'd explained her intention to wait for her wedding night to Keith, but he had never accepted her stand. Still, Andrea had been certain of their love, imagining Keith would get the message and propose to her.

The blinders had fallen from her eyes the fateful night she had eagerly anticipated a marriage proposal and had instead received a business proposition from the love of her life. That had been the end of everything. They had finished college without ever speaking another word to each other. She had married Jerrold O'Rourke—her sweet, sweet Jerry—six years later, and according to rumor, Keith had married about a year after that. His marriage had ended in divorce, hers by the terrible finality of death.

And now, after more years than she cared to add up, Keith was making overtures again? No, she would have no part of it. She didn't need or want his friendship, and she certainly could never want anything else from him. She would get through tonight and then retreat back into her own life. This foray into Keith's world would never be repeated. Never!

Andrea finally reached the parking area with its dozens upon dozens of cars. Veering right, she located the limousines and realized, to her dismay, they all looked alike. Her limo had been white, but most of them were white and she hadn't paid attention to exterior details.

Distraught and frowning, she stood there and wondered what to do next. Hearing footsteps behind her, she turned and saw Keith coming toward her. Instead of resenting his presence, she felt relief. Maybe *he* could identify the right limousine.

"Something wrong?" Keith called out before reaching her. He'd seen nothing at all of Dorian, thank goodness, and hoped again that the slime had left the ball and gone back under his rock.

"All of these limousines look alike," Andrea explained with a small frown.

Keith stopped next to her and studied the gleaming vehicles. "No, they don't. The one you arrived in is third from the left."

"It is?" Andrea peered at the one he'd named. To her it looked almost exactly like its neighbors, and she sighed. "I'll have to take your word for it." She started walking toward it. Keith kept stride—again—and she knew there was no shaking him tonight.

Keith opened the door of the limousine and peered inside. "I don't see a handbag," he said.

"Let me see." Andrea tried not to make contact as she moved around him, but felt the brush of their bodies as she peered inside. The distraction of the warmth he was emanating and her determination to ignore it made it difficult to focus on the task at hand. "I don't see it, either."

Turning a bit, she sat on the seat and began checking under it. Sliding along the soft leather seat she finally exclaimed, "Here it is! It must have fallen…" To her dismay, when she looked toward Keith, he wasn't patiently waiting at the door of the limousine, he was inside the car with her. "What on earth are you doing?" she demanded coldly.

"I *was* going to help you look for your bag."

"Well, I found it, so put your transmission in reverse!"

"I've got a better idea." He pulled the door shut and slid

her way in one fluid movement. ''The formal segment of the ball is going to get started in about ten minutes, but that's long enough for former sweethearts to renew old acquaintances, don't you agree?''

Two

To Andrea's surprise, the closed door merely piqued her curiosity. Certainly there was no reason to fear Keith. Goodness knows, he'd never had a vicious or threatening bone in his body, and in spite of old resentments she couldn't imagine him changing in that regard.

"Whatever could you be thinking?" she murmured.

Keith wasn't a bit bashful. "There's a lot on my mind tonight. For quite some time now. For certain since our last meeting."

"Which was when?" There was false innocence in her voice because she recalled the last time they'd seen each other quite clearly. She had been dining with a very nice young woman, Rebecca Todman, who had come to her for advice over Rebecca's abusive past. Andrea's longtime, well-known connection with New Hope sometimes resulted in one-on-one discussions with distraught women seeking relief from emotional pain and scarring caused by abusive relationships.

At any rate, Andrea had listened to Rebecca's story throughout most of the meal and was in the process of assuring her that she seemed to be on the road to healing herself when Keith and Robert Cole, the detective hired by Wescott Oil to investigate the murder of Eric Chambers, came into the restaurant. Andrea had seen their entrance but could not have imagined them joining her and Rebecca. Robert's interest in Rebecca had been the big draw, not anything between her and Keith. She'd been only cool and distant with him, as usual, she recalled now, so whatever tidbit of association occurring that evening to cause "a lot on his mind" had completely escaped her notice.

"Surely you remember," Keith said. "You were with Rebecca and…"

"Yes," she said flatly, cutting him off.

In truth she had absolutely no desire to know what had happened that evening to reactivate his interest in her. The mere thought of Keith in her life again was stupefying. Why, they couldn't be more different! He was wealthy beyond belief and while she was far from poverty—she had inherited from both of her parents and then her husband—her style of living would bore Keith silly. *His* would destroy her. Loud and boisterous friends, too much money and living in an ostentatious mansion? Oh no, she couldn't even think of that sort of existence without shuddering.

The limousine's interior lights had gone out when Keith closed the door, but the parking lot lights illuminated his face. Andrea looked straight into his eyes and asked, "Isn't it time we returned to the clubhouse? If I remember correctly, dinner is to start promptly at eight. I don't have a watch. What time is it?"

Keith obligingly checked his watch. "Yes, we have to go back, but in a minute. Andy—do you remember when I called you Andy?—for some time now when I've seen you something inside of me does flip-flops. I've been trying to understand it, without a whole lot of success. But since I have that same sensation tonight, it has to mean something. Any ideas?''

''One springs to mind,'' she said dryly. ''Flopping organs could be serious. I would contact my cardiologist and request an EKG if I were you.''

Keith grinned. ''Ouch.''

''Then again, it could be gas. Come on, let's go.''

Keith stared at her, admiring her grit and knowing he couldn't let her get away with such brazen repartee at his expense. He moved quickly but smoothly, taking her by surprise, and ended up with his arms around her and his mouth on hers. He felt her shocked gasp on his lips but instantly forgot it within the hot whirlwind of emotions overwhelming him. Her mouth was incredible, soft and sensuous, and while she wasn't exactly kissing him back, she wasn't trying to scratch out his eyes, either.

He didn't overdo it and broke the kiss after only a few moments. ''Dear Andy,'' he murmured softly. ''Sweet as candy. We had the real thing once, or we almost did. Something tells me that *this* is our time.''

She was so outraged that she was trembling. ''This is *not* our time! I don't even know what you mean by that absurdity. Let go of me, Keith.''

''Let's go inside and have some fun,'' he said cheerfully, letting her go.

''I'm afraid your idea of fun and mine do not coincide.'' Instead of waiting for him to get out through the door they both had used to gain entrance to the limousine, she opened the one on her side of the vehicle and exited as gracefully as she could manage, considering the explosive nature of her mood.

Keith hastened to join her. ''When did you become a snob?'' he asked.

Andrea stiffened and almost gave him no answer at all. How dare he judge her? But after a few seconds she *had* to defend herself. ''I am not a snob,'' she said icily.

"Sure you are. You think you're superior to everyone here, especially me. You didn't feel that way in college."

"That was twenty years ago! I don't know who or what I was in college, other than stupid!" She was referring, of course, to her relationship with him and hoping he got the message.

He did, but not precisely as she'd meant it. "It wasn't twenty years ago, it was eighteen years ago, and we were both a little stupid in those days. But neither of us was a snob, Andy Pandy."

"Please stop calling me those ridiculous names!"

"I like those names. Be honest. Didn't you enjoy that kiss just a little?"

They had reached the patio, which was completely vacant. Everyone had gone into the ballroom for dinner. Andrea stopped at the door to send him a very poisonous look.

"You are my age, thirty-eight years old, and still you be-have like an adolescent. No, Keith, I did not enjoy that kiss. Perhaps I liked being pawed in my youth, but *my* youth has long been spent. Apparently yours hasn't."

Swinging away, she opened the door for herself and went in. Shaking his head, Keith followed. "You act as though we're ready for the rocking chairs. You sure don't look like your nights should be spent a-rocking and a-reading. Hey, that's good. You used to rock and roll, and now you rock and read." He ducked his head to peer at her face. "Am I right or wrong?"

"What you are is incredibly vexing."

"Vexing? I'm vexing? You know, I've seen that word in novels but I've never heard anyone actually use it before. Vexing Keith." He chuckled. "Guess I'm a vexin' Texan."

"You're also not nearly as clever as you think you are."

"But I'm cute."

Andrea rolled her eyes. "Puppies, kittens and small chil-dren are cute. You're a middle-aged man, for pity's sake. Get over yourself."

"Middle-aged! Boy, you go right for the jugular, don't you? Now, that hurt, Dandy Andy."

"I hope so," she said sweetly and then said no more; they had reached the entrance to the ballroom. She could see that it had been festively decorated and set up for dinner with numerous tables, which were filled with chatting, excited, laughing people. Later, after dinner and the ceremony of presenting her with the club's donation, most of the tables would be removed to make room for dancing. Andrea planned to leave shortly thereafter, as soon as she could do so without appearing rude or ungrateful. She was, after all, representing New Hope, and she couldn't act solely on her own behalf. Of course, if she had only herself to consider, she wouldn't be here in the first place.

Keith offered his arm and said quietly, "Our table is across the room."

Gritting her teeth, Andrea forced herself to take his arm and to smile. Crossing that large room on Keith Owens's arm, with nearly every eye in the place on the two of them, was pure torture. She knew she shouldn't let it bother her. After all, she was there for the charity presentation, but how people did love to talk! To whisper and speculate and imagine. Andrea could see them doing it as she and her self-appointed escort moved among the tables. Escort indeed. What nerve!

"Here we are," Keith announced, stopping at a circular table with four couples and two vacant places. "I think you already know some of these people, but let's make this easy. Starting on the left we have Will and Diana Bradford, then Rob and Rebecca Cole, Sebastian and Susan Wescott and finally Jason and Merry Windover. Everyone, this lovely lady is Andrea O'Rourke."

Hellos were said, Andrea's chair was pulled out and then she and Keith sat down. Conversations began, and Andrea participated graciously. In mere minutes the first course of the meal was served, and Andrea found herself relaxing with these friendly people. From bits and pieces of the table talk she overheard while eating, she gathered that all of the men were members of the Cattleman's Club, which forced her to alter the hard-drinking, crude-talking, cigar-puffing image of the typical member of this club with which she'd arrived. These were intelligent, attractive people, every one of them, ranging in age from mid-twenties to early forties, and it occurred to Andrea that she could like them—some more than others, of course—if they weren't such bosom buddies with Keith.

She fell silent, while enjoying a delicious salad made with tender greens, warm mushrooms and crunchy pecans, and thought about the kiss he'd ambushed her with in the limousine. She was glad, of course, that she hadn't embarrassed herself by kissing him back. With his massive ego Keith would have taken even the slightest response from her as a green light and no telling what would have happened next.

Andrea suffered a sinking sensation over the scenario that idea conjured up. She knew *exactly* what would have happened if she had given Keith the encouragement he'd obviously hoped for. The problem with that relatively certain theory was the sensual ache it created in the pit of her stomach.

No! She would not ache for Keith Owens! For heaven's sake, had she lost her mind tonight? She *never* thought about sex. She wasn't looking for a man now, nor had she even considered another man since Jerry's death! *Lord love a duck, if you have to suddenly rediscover your libido, why pick Keith?*

Right in the middle of that horrifying question she felt Keith's leg press hers under the table. She moved her leg away from his and furtively reached under the tablecloth and pinched him on his nervy thigh, at the same time giving him a phony smile and saying in a low, for-his-ears-only voice, "Try that again and I'll sue you for sexual harassment. There are eight witnesses around this table, and friends of yours or not, if I suddenly stood up and told you to keep your hands to yourself, they would testify on my behalf in court."

"All I did was accidentally touch your leg with mine.

You're the one with the wandering hands. Who pinched whose thigh, you sneaky Pete?''

"Who kissed whom in the limousine, you Don Juan degenerate?''

"Oh, oh, the club photographer just snapped your picture. Could be one for the books, what with that accusing, vengeful expression on your pretty face.''

"You're lying through your teeth. I know how to maintain a normal expression however furious my thoughts.''

"Learn that trick during your marriage?''

Andrea gasped. "How dare you? My marriage was…was wonderful!''

"Yeah," Keith drawled. "So was mine. That's why I'm divorced.''

"You know perfectly well my husband passed away. We *never* would have gotten divorced!''

Keith regretted his comment at once. He never should have wisecracked about Andrea's marriage, not when he really knew nothing about it except that her husband had died. He just seemed to be more nervous around Andrea than he'd anticipated.

"I'm sorry," he said quietly. "I shouldn't have implied anything.''

"No, you should not have!" Andrea turned away. In a second she sent him another resentful look. "And I am not a snob. You're incredibly rude, which, when I recall the past, you always were.''

"Rude, vexing Keith," he whispered with a dramatic sigh. He had to get over it, he knew, and forced himself to lighten up and ask, "How did you ever put up with me for so many years?''

Andrea decided they were both going too far. If it hadn't been for the din of so many conversations plus background music, their dinner companions would already easily have overheard them. She didn't want to cause more gossip, since she was positive it was already occurring all around their table. It was better just to ignore Keith as much as she could.

Dishes were cleared away for the next course and Andrea looked up to see Laura Edwards, a waitress from the Royal Diner, working at another table. Laura wasn't a friend, but Andrea knew her from stopping into the diner occasionally to indulge in one of Manny, the cook's, fabulous hamburgers. The diner itself was an assault on one's senses with its red vinyl décor and smoke-stained walls and ceiling, but there was no question about Manny's burgers being the best in town.

Something about Laura tonight gave Andrea pause. The woman looked pale, pinched and—was *haunted* the right word for that wary, frightened expression on Laura's face? Or perhaps *hunted* was more appropriate. After a few moments of watching the waitress at work, and pondering her unusual demeanor, it occurred to Andrea that Laura looked exactly like the terrified women who came to New Hope's shelter to escape abuse!

Andrea pushed back her chair. "Please excuse me," she murmured to the table in general. Keith leaped up and the other men started to rise, also. Andrea smiled her thanks at them and walked toward the Ladies' Lounge sign. As planned, she intercepted Laura on her way to the kitchen with a tray of dirty dishes.

"Laura, hello," she said. "I'd like to speak to you. Can you take a minute?"

"Oh, Mrs. O'Rourke," Laura said in recognition. "It would have to be only a minute…we're all real busy…but let me get rid of this tray first."

"Of course. Can you meet me in the ladies' lounge?"

"Employees aren't supposed to use that facility, but I'll tell the boss that you asked to see me about something. That should clear it."

"Good. See you shortly." Andrea continued on to the lounge and Laura disappeared into the kitchen. Andrea was touching up her lipstick in front of a long beveled mirror over a pink marble counter—pink marble was the last thing she might have expected to see anywhere within the confines of this otherwise blatantly male retreat—when the door opened and Laura slipped silently into the room.

Andrea turned from the mirror. "Thanks. Laura, I can see from the look in your eyes and on your face that something is seriously wrong. I'm sure you're aware of my connection to New Hope and of the good the organization does for battered and abused women. You can talk to me, Laura. Nothing you say would ever be repeated, except perhaps to a counselor at the center, and only with your permission."

Laura was visibly squirming, obviously taken by surprise. "It…it's not that, Mrs. O'Rourke."

"Call me Andrea. I know how hard it is to talk about certain troubles, Laura, but if you're in an abusive relationship you really must get out of it. I can help. New Hope can help."

Laura wouldn't quite meet her eyes and something sighed within Andrea. It happened so often. Too many abused women simply couldn't speak of their torment and suffering until it got too horrible to bear. Andrea couldn't spot any bruises on Laura, but some men beat their women in places that were ordinarily covered by clothing. And then, too, emotional bruising wasn't visible.

Andrea reached into her small handbag for a business card, which she put in Laura's hand. "Please call me if you ever need to talk, Laura," she said gently. "Along with New Hope's number, my home number is on this card. Call anytime, day or night."

"Thank you," Laura said hoarsely, slipping the card into a pocket of her uniform. "I…I really have to get back to work."

"I understand." Andrea smiled. "I wish I knew what to say to put a smile on your face."

"You're a kind person." Laura smiled a little before hurrying out.

Andrea sighed again. That wan, mirthless smile that Laura had attempted spoke volumes, but the subject matter could only be guessed at. Obviously the woman was miserably unhappy over something, but was that something a man? An *abusive* man?

Leaving the ladies' lounge, Andrea returned to her table.

Three hours later Keith walked her to the waiting limousine. The check made out to New Hope Charity in Andrea's purse was such a generous sum that she had let its many zeroes influence her normal good judgment and had stayed at the ball much longer than she'd intended. Yes, she had even danced, with Keith and with several other men, and she regretted playing the social butterfly now because Keith was insistent about seeing her home.

"I'll just ride along, walk you to your door to make sure you get home safe and sound, and then leave."

Keith had been honestly concerned about Dorian forcing that introduction to Andrea, although Dorian must have left immediately after. Keith had watched all evening for him and had also alerted his friends to Dorian's presence and intrusion, so they'd been watching, as well. But just because he'd vanished from the ball didn't lessen Keith's concern about Andrea going home alone.

She, of course, only saw Keith's insistence as more attention than she wanted from him. "Please," she said. "I'm exhausted and I don't need anyone walking me to my door. I've lived alone for five years. I go home by myself after dark all the time."

"Well, maybe you shouldn't."

"Nonsense." Andrea extended her hand for a handshake. "Let's say good-night here, and thank you again for a most generous donation."

His dark eyes bored into her. "I'd rather kiss you than shake your hand."

She sucked in a sudden sharp breath. "Don't, Keith! You and I are *not* going to take up where we left off twenty years ago."

"Eighteen years, and why aren't we? Give me ten good reasons."

"I'll give you *one*. I don't want to. Good night." Andrea got into the limousine, the chauffeur closed the door and hurried around to the driver's door, and they drove off. Andrea looked out the back window and saw Keith standing there, watching, just watching. He looked disappointed and…worried? Why on earth would he be worrying about her?

Turning around to face front, she put her head back and told herself that she didn't care what was going on with him. They weren't friends or lovers, merely very old acquaintances, and she had absolutely no desire to change the status quo. He had his world, she had hers, and it was best that they each stay within the boundaries they had been living within for many years. Why he would suddenly want to cross over into her world, or coax her into his after so long was beyond her.

She only knew she couldn't let it happen.

Keith stood there until the limousine's taillights were out of sight, then avoided the clubhouse and the valet, and walked to the parking lot to get his car for himself. It was much cooler at midnight than it had been earlier and the fresh night air felt good to him. Even so, he walked with his head down.

The night had not gone as well as he'd hoped. Dorian's appearance had put everyone that knew the score on edge, of course, but even without that, Keith wasn't satisfied with the evening—all due to Andrea's adamant refusal to let down her guard with him. There was a wall around her that he hadn't been able to breach with teasing good humor, open and admitted admiration or a pass he probably shouldn't have made. It was odd how differently each of them saw the past. Possibly they'd been in love in college, but he couldn't be sure. His head had been so full of ambitious dreams and he'd honestly believed Andrea had felt the same way. Even now Keith was positive they hadn't been ready for the responsibilities of marriage back then; there were too many things to be done before taking that particular step.

Still, there had always been a serious connection between them, from their toddler sandbox days to that first experimental kiss and on through the rigors of high school. It was during the summer following high-school graduation, Keith recalled, that they had begun seeing each other as adults. And then in college they had gotten closer still. If it had been up to him they would have spent most of their free time in bed. Damn, he'd wanted her! Andrea was the one who'd kept things cool between them, but hadn't her attitude been rather childish? After all, they had ended up in a horrific fight that had completely destroyed what they'd had, and, thinking about it now, Keith couldn't help blaming Andrea's stubborn insistence on chastity as the cause of their breakup.

Oh, well, he thought with a heavy sigh as he reached his car and got into it. Tearing apart the past was useless. He needed to concentrate on the present, on his campaign to prove Dorian's guilt and on what he was going to do about Andrea now. They were completely separate issues, but each was seriously crucial to Keith's peace of mind.

He simply was not going to accept Andrea's avoidance any longer, that was all there was to it. Andy Vance O'Rourke was going to learn that he could be every bit as stubborn as she was, and what's more, he was going to have fun in the process.

And so was she. Seeing her tonight, watching her so closely, sensing her withdrawal from anything that didn't measure up to whatever high-handed rules she lived by had told him that she needed some fun in her life. Some *real* fun.

He was the guy to provide it, the guy to make her laugh and love and enjoy herself.

He knew it in his soul.

Andrea had an awful time sleeping that night, or what was left of it. She came wide awake at six the next morning, lay in her bed tired and resentful for an hour, then got up and stood under the shower until her head felt clearer.

Usually she ran in the morning. Rarely did a morning pass,

in fact, that she didn't run at least three miles. Her route took her from Pine Valley, Royal's upscale community in which she and nearly everyone who could afford it had their home, to Royal Park, which had a well-used hiking trail completely surrounding it. A couple of turns around that trail and then the return trip to Pine Valley added up to three miles, a good workout.

It bothered Andrea that Keith lived in Pine Valley, too, although his mansion was on Millionaire's Row, as that one particular area of Pine Valley was called by those in the know, and her house was quite some distance away. But she'd always known where he lived, even when she'd purchased her home, so she had eventually taken his presence—albeit mostly invisible—in stride.

Her house was lovely, small by Pine Valley standards, but very cozy and homey. It was a typical rancher but with lots of bells and whistles. After Jerry's death she had sold the house they'd lived in during their marriage and bought this one. It would never do for a family, but it was perfect for one or two people. She had decorated it exactly to her liking, the very first time she'd been able to do that, and the interior colors were soft and conducive to peaceful relaxation.

This Sunday morning Andrea felt neither peaceful nor relaxed. She didn't want to run, either. She was restless, barely able to sit still for more than a minute, but running held no appeal today, and these were very uncommon feelings for her to have. She knew who to blame for her unusual edginess.

How dared Keith kiss her last night? Memories of the entire evening seemed to bombard her from every direction.

It was noon before she felt halfway normal again, before she was calm enough to phone the officers of New Hope and relate the amount of the Texas Cattleman's Club's donation. They were, of course, overjoyed.

After that Andrea went back to bed, ignored several telephone calls that she let her voice mail pick up and spent a perfectly miserable afternoon switching channels on the large-screen television set in her bedroom.

It appeared that Keith Owens was succeeding in ruining her life, just as she'd feared would be the case if she were ever nice to him even one time.

Keith's Sunday was almost as unproductive as Andrea's, the main difference being the time he spent in searching the files in Eric Chambers's computer. Keith had brought the computer home rather than to his company office, as he wanted the club members' interest in this whole sad affair to remain as low-key as possible. That was the way the men of the club that were involved in saving lives and/or bringing criminals to justice worked—discreetly, strategically, invisibly.

The computer's hard disk was laden with accounting files, understandable since Eric had been vice president of accounting at Wescott Oil. But there were numerous sub-files with far more information about clients of Wescott Oil than Keith thought necessary, indicating to him that Eric had been obsessive about detail. Nowhere, however, were there any notations or entries regarding the missing money. Considering Eric's penchant for detail, Keith thought that strange.

After hours of searching, he opened Eric's personal journal file and looked for hidden attachments. He could find nothing more than Rob had, but that didn't satisfy Keith. He was positive that he had to be missing something, and he wasn't giving up on finding it after only one session. Still, he turned off the computer, got to his feet and stretched his back.

For the rest of the evening he thought about the ball and Andrea. Just as he couldn't give up on cracking Eric's computer secrets, neither could he give up on Andrea just because she hadn't encouraged his interest last night.

And he had an idea of what to do next to get her attention, too. He only hoped it would work.

Three

The following morning, a Monday, Andrea was back to normal except for one thing. She was thoroughly disgusted with herself for having wasted a beautiful day in June in maudlin self-denouncement and angry resentment of Keith. Ignoring church services and friends' telephone calls were things she just didn't do, and there were messages on her voice mail to remind her of yesterday's outlandishly childish behavior.

She did her running with a determined, almost grim expression on that sunny Monday morning, even while enjoying the diamond-like sparkle of dew on grass and flowers, and the fresh air. Running was one of her greatest pleasures and she was not going to allow Keith Owens to destroy the contentment of her daily routines. There was no reason ever to see him again, except by the whims of chance. Should another occasion such as the charity ball arise she would simply refuse to participate.

Andrea loved Royal Park with its little lake, botanical garden and striking gazebo that had been the center of many

Fourth of July celebrations. This was a park that was actually used, and even at this early hour she could see people walking, jogging or sitting on benches near the lake, some of them feeding the resident ducks.

After several turns around the park, Andrea headed for home. Sweaty, but feeling more at peace with herself, she entered her house and went straight to her shower. Twenty minutes later, she scanned the morning paper while eating fresh fruit and cold cereal for her breakfast. She tidied the kitchen, her bedroom and bathroom, then got dressed, choosing a simply styled blue-and-white cotton dress and flat shoes. Her hair was almost dry and she fluffed it slightly, applied makeup very sparingly, ignored perfume and cologne and decided she would do.

Taking up her workday purse, she located her car keys and used the connecting door between laundry and garage. Because she drove slowly with the windows down—very soon it would be much too hot to drive anywhere without the vehicle's air conditioner going full blast—and enjoyed the activity of the town, it took her a good fifteen minutes to reach Kiddie Kingdom, the nursery school at which she taught. Like New Hope Charity, the nursery school was situated in a very old house that had once been quite charming. Now its high-ceilinged rooms were used as classrooms for preschool children, and its once elegant backyard was a playground with swing sets, a sturdy slide and a merry-go-round. Huge ancient oaks shaded the play area, so even on the hottest days youngsters could spend some time outdoors.

Andrea's charges were three- and four-year-olds, wee boys and girls that she absolutely adored. Following college Andrea had taught fifth- and sixth-graders, and after her marriage she'd taken on some high-school classes, which had been quite an experience. Most teenage students, she had discovered, were bright, intelligent, witty and sweet, but some were so difficult and rude that Andrea had been forced to change her idealistic belief that no child was unteachable. She'd changed her tune after that and gone back to teaching youngsters. Now she couldn't be happier with her position. She wasn't working for the modest paycheck but because she loved children, and there was nothing more satisfying for her than watching them learn and knowing she was part of their expanding knowledge.

She and Jerry had both wanted children of their own, but none came along and they went in for testing. The tests revealed Jerry's sterility, along with a list of other medical conditions, including a weakened heart. Jerry had always avoided doctors so diligently that he honestly hadn't known that his aches and pains—everyone had 'em, so why stress over it? he'd always said with an infectious laugh—were signs of severe physical breakdown. But Jerry hadn't changed his stubborn ways just because of a serious diagnosis. He had worked as hard as ever, played tennis like a wild man and done anything else he'd pleased regardless of doctors' recommendations that he slow down and conduct both work and play at a less hectic pace.

Andrea had been more furious than grief-stricken when he had simply keeled over one day. He could have lived a much longer life—possibly into old age—had he listened to his doctors. But Jerry had been Jerry, and she'd loved him for his Irish wit, strength and temperament. No one had ever gotten away with telling him what to do, not his family, not the medical community, not her, even though Andrea knew he'd loved her with all his heart.

Finally she had tucked away her grief and built a life without him. She'd done a pretty good job of it, too, she felt. Until last Saturday night, that is.

No, she was not going to think of that again, she decided vehemently while entering her classroom and putting away her purse. The children were arriving, delivered to Kiddie Kingdom by parents or nannies.

"Good morning, Natalie," she said to a tiny blond girl, who responded with a shy little smile.

And so it went, as did every weekday morning. Andrea greeted each child by name as he or she came in, and when everyone had arrived she began the day's lessons. Teaching such young children was best accomplished in short segments, with songs and games interspersed among the lessons. Remarkably, some of these tots could already read. Others were just beginning to learn the alphabet. Andrea gave as much one-on-one attention to the children as she could squeeze into their three-hour school day, which to her seemed to fly by.

It was around ten-thirty when the door to her classroom opened and in walked Keith Owens, dressed in tan chinos and a casual, white, open-at-the-neck shirt. Andrea was so startled that she gaped at him with her mouth open. He smiled broadly, as though she shouldn't be at all surprised to see him, walked to the back of the room and sat on one of the tiny chairs provided for the pupils. He looked ridiculous to Andrea, but worse than that in her eyes, every one of the children had turned around to stare at him. He looked back at them unabashedly, with a friendly sort of half grin, and Andrea soon began seeing smiles on their little faces.

Clearing her throat, clinging to composure through sheer will power, she walked to where he was sitting, bent forward and whispered, "What's going on? What are you doing here?"

"I'm just visiting, so don't enroll me," he said with a devilish twinkle in his eyes.

"How cute," she said coldly. "You're a distraction. Please leave," she added, refusing to laugh at his feeble excuse for a joke.

"A distraction? For whom?"

"For the *children!* Get off that chair before you break it…and leave!"

"Nope."

It occurred to her that he might have a child. She didn't know *everything* about him, after all, and since she had never encouraged anyone to talk about him, it was possible that he and his ex-wife had children that she hadn't heard about.

"Do you have a child to enroll?" she asked bluntly.

"No, do you?"

Her heart seemed to flip in her chest. She'd wanted kids so much, and teaching these adorable tots satisfied some of her need to nurture, but not all of it. At that moment she hated Keith more than she had when they'd fought and broken up in college.

"You *know* I don't," she whispered harshly.

Keith could tell he'd struck a nerve, which wasn't his intention. He'd been hoping that she would laugh over his coming to Kiddie Kingdom and perching on a child-size chair. Didn't Andrea laugh at anything anymore? "Sorry," he murmured. "I'd like to watch the class for a while."

"Even if your presence is a distraction for the children?"

"It's bothering you a lot more than it is them, Teach," he said softly. If he let her chase him off every time he appeared, he'd *never* get anywhere with her. And he wanted to, very much, even if he really didn't comprehend why.

Andrea realized he wasn't going to budge. In no position to show her anger, she pivoted on her heel and returned to the front of the classroom. She did her best to ignore Keith while reciting the alphabet with the class, reading a story out loud and passing out cartons of juice, but she was almost lethally aware of him every second.

At recess time she led the children out to the playground, and when she brought them inside again about twenty minutes later, Keith was gone.

It didn't seem to matter. He had succeeded in turning her inside out once again, and when it was time to go home for the day, she felt totally drained. Andrea drove home with a very suspicious mist in her eyes, and she hated the possibility that she was crying over Keith Owens again. Hadn't she cried enough tears because of him eighteen years ago?

Pulling herself together, she stopped at the bank and deposited the check in New Hope's account, the usual routine with donations that she or other volunteers personally received. Tucking the receipt in her purse so she could later pass it to the charity's accountant, she returned to her car.

Underway again, her thoughts immediately returned to Keith's unmitigated gall that morning.

That *had* been a one-time intrusion, hadn't it?

Andrea's breath nearly stopped. Surely he wouldn't be back!

But what if he did come back? Maybe she should talk to the principal, but what on earth would she say? *Keith Owens is visiting my classroom and driving me up the wall. Would you please do something about it?*

Visitors were not unwelcome at Kiddie Kingdom. Besides, should principal Nancy Pringle take Andrea's complaint seriously and talk to Keith the next time he showed up—*if* he came by again—he would have Nancy tittering and tee-heeing all over the place with his good looks and glib way of conversing with women. Andrea saw through him, but would Nancy? Oh, he would undoubtedly charm his way out of any accusation Andrea made against him, make no mistake.

So if he *did* show up again, she was going to have to grin and bear it, Andrea thought with a groan of frustration. In the next instant, however, she switched from frustrated to furious. She might have to bear Keith's presence until he grew bored with the little game he was playing, but she didn't have to be nice to him and she was not going to be! He'd catch on. He might be a pain in the neck but he wasn't stupid. He'd get tired of being ignored very quickly.

Feeling much better, Andrea pulled into her garage, got out of the car and went into the house. Deciding that she needed something to take her mind off of Keith, she prepared some lunch then sat at the glass-topped kitchen table with a pad and pen. She had always enjoyed planning a dinner party, and by the time she finished eating she had five names on her pad, along with the start of a wonderful menu.

Since this was an impromptu affair for the coming Friday evening, she phoned her friends rather than send written invitations, which was a nicety to which she normally adhered. Delighted that everyone accepted on such short notice, Andrea fluffed out the skeleton menu with some especially delicious side dishes, added two desserts, one made completely of fresh fruit and the other a decadently rich strawberry mousse served in a flaky pastry crust.

She occupied herself for another thirty minutes with a grocery list, which she would fill on Friday afternoon, then sat and stared blankly through one of the tall, undraped windows that framed the splendor of her yard on three sides of the kitchen's dining nook. A wide overhang shaded every window in the house, which allowed Andrea to leave curtains, shutters, drapes and blinds open, if she wished.

But she wasn't enjoying the view of evenly trimmed grass and symmetrically perfect beds of flowers as she ordinarily did. She felt blue and lonely, she realized unhappily, and even anticipation of Friday's dinner party—already a success because everyone had eagerly accepted her invitation—couldn't dispel the terrible aloneness gnawing at her.

The sensation frightened and then angered her, because feeling like the last rose of summer was not her fault. Something she'd been fighting against believing was suddenly too clear and real to thrust aside any longer: Keith had, for some unknown reason, decided to become a part of her life again. Just how far he wanted to take this new and extremely perturbing admiration of her she could only guess at, but she could hardly assume he only intended them to be on friendly speaking terms when he'd kissed her at the first opportunity. So what did he want, an affair?

Andrea's stomach began churning in alarm. An affair was so...so...well, it was something she'd never done and just the thought of making love with Keith made her feel shaky and weak. Actually she suddenly felt like going to bed and hiding again, as she'd done yesterday, but she told herself to stop it at once. *You cannot run to your bedroom every time Keith and what he might want from you pops into your silly head!*

Feeling like a total mess—a rare sensation for Andrea—

she dragged herself to her feet and forced herself to clear away the dishes she'd used for lunch.

The next morning Keith was back. Andrea felt her knees go weak when he strolled into the classroom as though he owned the school, the town and all of Texas. No one could ever say that Keith Owens lacked self-confidence, which, at the moment, didn't make her like him any better.

But, sad to say, even while disliking him intensely—or telling herself she did—she felt his magnetism even more than she had at the ball. And she'd let him kiss her that night! How far might she let him go?

Shaking her head to rid her brain of such nonsense, Andrea went on with the story she'd been reading before Keith's interruption. It was about frogs and turtles and a small boy on a farm, a sweet, well-written little story that the children had been enthralled with before Keith walked in. Now they were more interested in the big man sitting on the tiny chair at the back of the room.

Andrea said in the gentle way she spoke to her class, "Children, look at me, please." The little faces turned to her again. "Mr. Owens, unfortunately, was not allowed to attend nursery school when he was your age, and he came here yesterday and again today to learn all of the lovely things you are learning. But we shouldn't stare at him, should we? Staring is very impolite. Just think of him as another class-mate...a much taller classmate, of course...but one who is about the same age as you are. Can you do that?"

Keith almost burst out laughing. Andrea's putting him in his place, cutting him down to size for intruding on her class, had surprised him. He gulped back waves of rolling laughter and decided again that he *had* to bring them together. Hell's bells, their past was so long ago it shouldn't matter to either of them now. They hadn't parted on friendly terms, true, but this was another lifetime. She was an intelligent woman, and while she was obviously wary of his intentions, she couldn't possibly still be holding a grudge after so many years.

"I'm five," a small boy boasted proudly.

"Not yet, Jason," Andrea said with a warm smile. "Next month, I believe? Yes, I'm sure of it. Your birthday is in July and *then* you will be five. Class, would you like to hear the rest of the story?"

"Yes," the tots all shouted.

"Very well." Andrea began reading again. At times during the story she was so aware of Keith's eyes on her that the fine hairs on the back of her neck prickled. She *had* to stop him from coming here, but how? What could she possibly do that would chase him off, yet appear sensible and necessary to anyone else?

After recess, Keith disappeared again, and Andrea breathed more easily for the remainder of the morning. After parents or nannies had picked up the children, she put away toys and books to tidy her classroom then gathered her purse and left the building. Another teacher walked out with her and remarked on the great weather they were having.

Andrea smiled and agreed. They stopped and chatted for a few minutes about their individual classes and the children they were teaching—there were always anecdotes to relate to other teachers at the school—then they went in different directions to reach their vehicles in the parking lot. Andrea could feel her face turning crimson when she spotted Keith leaning against the back of her car, but she wasn't sure if her high, hot color was caused by anger or by a large spurt of adrenaline associated with unexpected, instantaneous and extremely shocking sexual awareness.

You've lived a celibate life far too long a time if just the sight of Keith can do this to you. And you thought you had every phase of your life under control, you...you dolt. Pull yourself together this instant! Don't you dare humiliate yourself by letting him know how strongly he affects you. He's already unbearably full of himself. Don't give him more fuel to feed his massive ego, for goodness sake!

Andrea's cheeks might be pink, but the expression on her

face could not have been frostier when she walked past Keith without a word and unlocked the driver's door of her car.

"Good afternoon to you, too," Keith said teasingly while ambling toward her.

She whirled on him. "You know something? I'm glad you hung around today because there are a few things I'd like to say to you."

Keith nodded. "Good, glad to hear it. I've got a whole bunch of things I'd like to say to you, too, but how about us talking over dinner tonight? We could go to Claire's, or to any other place you'd like. We could even drive to Midland, if you prefer."

"If I prefer? If I *prefer?* You…you…" She stopped her furious outburst and took a calming breath. After a moment she said, "Please listen to me. I don't know why you suddenly decided to annoy me by intruding on my classroom, but…"

Keith broke in. "Andrea, the answer to that couldn't be easier. I wanted to see you. It's as simple as that."

"Do you actually believe that becoming an irritating pest is going to make me like you?"

"Are you saying you *don't* like me? Andrea, you like everyone. Or you used to. You've become a snob of course, so I guess that changes things, but you have no reason to dislike me."

"No reason? You obviously have a conveniently selective memory, nice for you but selfish as all get-out for everybody else."

"Andrea, I've never been selfish with anything," Keith said, because he could see that Andrea was just barely managing to keep her temper in check. In fact the blazing blue light in her eyes truly surprised him; he believed that time healed wounds, real or imagined, big or small, and God knows, eighteen years was a long time.

"Do you actually believe that?" she demanded with astonishment.

"Yes…I do. Look, I realize now that getting the two of

us back together isn't going to be as easy as I'd thought. Or hoped. You've obviously got resentments to put to rest, but don't *you* realize nothing will be put to rest for either of us if we don't try? Have dinner with me. Lay your cards on the table. Andy, take the first step with me.''

''Oh, Lordy,'' she whispered, turning her face away to avoid seeing the plea in his dark eyes. Gathering her courage, she looked at him again. ''I have no cards, nor do you. Any step I would take with you would detour my life into unknown territory that I do not wish to explore. It may be impossible for you to understand, but I have not been living an unhappy existence. My life is full and I'm a contented woman. Or I was. You seem to be doing your level best to upset my personal applecart, and if I resent anything about you, Keith, it's that. Now, please leave me alone.''

She got in her car, started the motor, checked to make sure he'd moved out of the way, then backed out of her parking place and drove away.

Try as she might, she could not rid her mind of the look on his face when she'd delivered her final statement. Had it been cruel? No, she decided, not cruel, merely honest.

After all, how much pussyfooting could a woman do around a man she didn't want? *Even if he does fan old, all-but-forgotten embers back to life? Especially* if he fans old embers back to life, she thought adamantly. A fiery affair at her age was unthinkable. She was a lady, for God's sake, not a…a…

She stopped that thought before it got out of hand because she could not condemn women for making love. That sort of thing just wasn't for her; that was really all there was to it.

That philosophy did raise one question, however. If the man pursuing her with such determination weren't Keith Owens, would she be less strict about her personal code of ethics and morality?

Keith called a meeting at the club late that afternoon. When everyone had arrived and gone to one of the private rooms, Jason said as they got settled, "Something must have happened."

"Nothing conclusive," Keith replied. "Yet. But I've been going through Eric's computer with a fine-tooth comb and I found one totally unidentifiable file. There's nothing in it but numbers."

"Rob missed that?" Jason said, looking surprised.

"Rob did a darned good job, Jason. This particular file is not in any way connected to Eric's personal journal. It was and is attached to an accounting file and is obviously written in some sort of code. I printed it out so y'all could have a look at it." Keith went into the briefcase he'd brought and stashed next to his chair and came out with a sheaf of papers, which he passed around.

Sebastian spoke first, after studying the pages of numbers. "Is this a crackable code, Jason? With your CIA background, you must know something about codes."

"Any code is crackable," Jason said. "But not always easily nor by just anybody. We might be able to figure it out ourselves, or we might not. Should we bring in an expert?"

"I think we should give it a try first," Will said. "What do y'all think?" he asked, including every man in the circle of chairs in his question. "We're not cryptographers, but neither are we stupid. It's possible that we might make some sense out of this. And we've only used outside help in the past when absolutely necessary. If we're to maintain our practice of total privacy, we should only call on outsiders as a last resort."

"Will's right," Keith said. "I'd like each one of you to study those numbers and see if they make any sense. I've already thought of bank account numbers, but that idea was easily disproved. I believe it's a numerical code, with numbers representing letters or words or something else that can be transposed into words."

"Eric was a damned good accountant," Sebastian said, "but this is a pretty complex code..."

"Yes, I know what you mean," Keith said thoughtfully. "But, Sebastian, what's accounting if not numbers?"

Four

Keith sat in his favorite chair in the den, sipping an excellent cognac and staring into the gas-log flames of the fireplace. The fire wasn't needed for heat nor was it throwing enough to notice, but Keith enjoyed dancing flames with his cognac and troubled thoughts.

Eric's numeric code gnawed at him, but at the moment, questions about Andrea took precedence. Had he really loved her in college and been too beset with ambition to assign importance to anything else? Well, of course he'd loved her. He'd loved her for as long as he'd known her, since they were children. But had he also loved her in that special way a man loves the woman with whom he wants to spend the rest of his life?

Frowning at the fire, Keith raised his snifter for another taste of cognac.

Then there was another question: Were his feelings for Andrea the underlying reason his marriage had failed? Candace had always told him his mind was somewhere else. He had attributed her complaints to his work ethic, which truly had driven him back then. It was one of the ironies of his life, he felt, because these days one would be hard-pressed to locate that same quality of ambition within Keith Owens in any way, shape or form, all because of money. He'd become so wealthy from his computer software company that striving to increase that wealth seemed almost obscene. He rarely showed up at his business anymore; he had the best talent available in every key position, and he honestly didn't know if it was good or bad but he couldn't doubt that his former burning ambition had waned almost to the point of indifference. He'd changed, obviously, changed a lot, and if he and Candace were married now they might have made it to old age together.

That was neither here nor there, though. Candace was long gone—she was the person who had rejoiced in this huge mansion and the one who'd spent a fortune and the first year of their marriage decorating it—and Keith never really missed her. She'd had some good points, of course; he couldn't hate her for demanding a divorce and an enormous property settlement from a husband who'd given her anything money could buy but precious little time and consideration. She'd grown weary of it all, as he had, and finally there'd been nothing between them but anger, reproach and bickering.

And all the while, without trying, without ever going out of his way for information, he'd kept track of Andrea. Running into her on the street or in a shop had disturbed him in ways he hadn't let himself explore, for she'd never been anything but cold and distant. Her marriage had set him back a pace, though and then later on, the death of Jerry O'Rourke had been a major shock. He'd sent a huge flower arrangement to the funeral home and a sympathy card to Andrea's house, on which he'd personally written, ''I'm so very sorry. Please let me know if I can do anything to help you through this.''

He'd received a formal thank-you card for the flowers and

nothing else; she had never acknowledged his sympathy and offer of help in any way.

Narrowing his eyes thoughtfully, still gazing at the fire, Keith again sipped his brandy. He could not regret his behavior during his college years. He'd been young, overflowing with exciting plans, absolutely unstoppable physically—running on very little sleep and barely noticing it—and living on a natural high so incredible that remembering it brought tears to his eyes.

He didn't live on that plane of youthful exuberance now and he was able to spot the flaws that had totally eluded him at the time. For one thing, it was entirely possible that he'd let his soul mate, his mirror image in many ways, the one woman in all the world born perfect for him, as he was for her, get away.

Recalling their college relationship, the laughs, the gang of friends they'd happily shared and finally their private times, their kisses and petting sessions, was depressing for Keith, because they'd been in complete harmony on every issue but one. Andrea would *not* permit sex between them. She had kissed him, told him she loved him, let him caress her and touched him intimately. But when things got to that fever pitch, she stopped everything. He'd begged, debated with her even, ridiculed her righteous attitude and nothing had worked. She had been determined to be a virgin on her wedding night and she probably had been.

Only, he hadn't been the lucky groom.

Muttering a curse under his breath, Keith turned his thoughts to his present courtship. Was it working at all? Was he making Andrea remember their good times, as he couldn't help doing?

She was incredible with those kids in her class, he mused, picturing her gentle way of speaking to them, the warm and wonderful smiles she bestowed upon them. In the past, hadn't she talked about kids quite a lot? Yes, he was sure of it. Andrea had wanted a big family; he could recall her saying those very words many times. She'd been an only child, same

as him, and she had mourned her lack of siblings while growing up. Keith couldn't visualize her changing her mind on
something that had been so consistently momentous to her,
so *why* hadn't she had the family she'd so passionately
dreamed of producing?

He, on the other hand, had never yearned for kids and
neither had Candace. They'd been like-minded on that subject, if no other. He had spent precious little time in the
company of kids of any age. Certainly he'd never classified
noisy *small* people as either cute or smart. Those youngsters
in Andrea's class were unquestionably adorable—he'd never
even come close to an observation of that sort before, and
yes, it was surprising. It was also obvious that Andrea loved
each and every one of the tots in her class, so again, why
hadn't she had kids of her own?

Keith finally had to admit that furtively keeping track of
Andrea for eighteen years had never given him the kind of
personal information he would like to have about her now.
For instance, had she truly loved Jerry O'Rourke?

"Damn!" Keith exclaimed in sudden and startling frustration. Rising from his chair, he went to the fireplace and
turned off the gas. Then he took his brandy glass to the
kitchen and set it on the counter. Gabriella, his housekeeper
who came in every weekday morning, would rinse the glass
and put it in the dishwasher. It honestly never occurred to
him to do that simple chore himself. She kept the house spar-
kling clean and also did some cooking. There were always
casseroles, soups or stews in the refrigerator or freezer that
he could warm up should he decide to eat at home, which
was happening more and more of late. Keith had been raised
with housekeepers, cooks, gardeners, et cetera, and he'd hired
Gabriella to run his household as soon as he'd had a household to run. Candace had liked her, so Gabriella had been
around a long time.

Keith climbed the spectacular circular stairway in the massive foyer of his home to the second floor and went to the
large elegant master suite and ultimately to bed. Lying in the

dark with his hands behind his head, he came to a decision. He couldn't let Andrea's objections stop him. Not yet, at any rate. She was still ticked over their breakup, which seemed utterly ridiculous after so long a time, but women were funny about things that men barely noticed.

So, he'd give her as much time and as many opportunities as she needed to come around to his way of thinking. It would happen, he was positive. She was too intelligent to carry a silly grudge to the grave.

Smiling in self-satisfaction over his decision, Keith turned on his side, got comfortable in his oversize bed and closed his eyes.

Andrea sighed when Keith walked into her classroom yet again. Had he completely lost his former pride, which she recalled as stiff-necked and a seemingly indestructible part of him? She pondered the past and present in genuine and most definitely unamused amazement. Could she have made her disapproval of his ridiculous behavior any clearer yesterday? If someone had made it so plain that she wasn't wanted, she certainly would not have returned the very next day.

Keith touched the tips of his fingers to his forehead in an informal salute and smiled at her. Andrea tensed defensively, and she did *not* smile back. Actually, she longed to throw the storybook in her hand at him as he made his way to the back of the room and that tiny chair. What in heaven's name was she going to do about this? It was all up to her, for she could not complain about it to anyone. Keith was a well-known, highly respected person in Royal, and the only thing complaining would do was to spread the news that he was hot on her trail.

The children, she noticed then, had grown tired of staring at Keith and were beginning to squirm. She had been getting ready to read to them, thus the book in her hand, and inspiration suddenly struck.

"Children," she said calmly. "How would you like Mr. Owens to read to you today?"

"Yay!" they shouted, creating a din of high-pitched child-ish voices that could have jangled adult nerves within moments if Andrea had not quieted her tiny students.

Keith knew he'd been had. In fact, there was something about this sneaky tactic of Andrea's that smacked of polite warfare. It was if she'd thrown down a gauntlet, or fired the first shot. Oddly, what Keith perceived as a declaration of war didn't anger him in the least. Rather, it exhilarated him, awakened youthful energy that obviously—and happily—was still a part of him but that must have been in slumber mode.

With one eyebrow cocked and a devilish light gleaming in his dark eyes, he strolled to the front of the room. Andrea held out the book and he took it from her fingers. Before he even looked at it, he said, too quietly for the children to hear, "I accept your challenge."

"My what?" Confusion beset Andrea.

"You always did look good enough to eat…make that kiss…when you blushed. Now, let's take a look at this book."

Andrea wanted to wind up and sock him a good one. He aggravated her normal composure and stirred her anger much as a tornado shatters any earthly thing on which it descends.

"It was written for preschoolers, so I'm sure you'll be able to understand it," she said icily.

"Hmm," Keith murmured while perusing the cover art. "Yes," he added in a serious vein, "I probably will. Well, shall we get started?"

"Sit over there," Andrea told him, indicating the chair she always used when reading to the class. While Keith complied, she sat behind her desk. He began reading and the children stared wide-eyed at him.

Keith came to the phrase, "And the chicken said 'cluck, cluck, cluck,'" and each tiny child listening so spellbound shouted, "Cluck, cluck, cluck!" Startled, Keith looked over to Andrea for help, but she appeared to be writing something and was completely unaware of his quandary.

He figured it out for himself, though, when the pig in the story said, "Oink, oink, oink," and the children shouted the "oinks" as he read them. *These little ones know this story by heart!* From that moment on Keith began enjoying himself. He oinked and whinnied and clucked and mooed, and when the kids giggled because he sounded so funny, he laughed with them.

Andrea kept her pen in her hand, but she was watching Keith and the kids very closely. She'd never seen him with small children before, but the Keith she'd known in college would not have had one second of fun reading to them. He especially would not have done or said anything to make anyone—even small children—laugh at him!

She felt something shriveling within herself; it was her years-long resentment of Keith and it quickly diminished to a barely recognizable mass. *You're getting mushy and soft just because he's having fun with the kids, and they like him? Don't be a fool, Andrea. He's still the same man who broke your heart in college.*

From out of nowhere came a painful, unfamiliar urge to weep. Not to sob or bawl but to quietly weep for things that might have been. The feeling unnerved her. Her life had been good. Her life *was* good. She'd married a wonderful man, and Jerry would always hold a special place in her heart. She had good health, this job she loved, great friends and enough financial security to live comfortably for the rest of her days. And still she felt like weeping because a man who had no right at all to intrude on her safe, secure little world was making her tiny students laugh and clap their hands.

Andrea held back the tears, but her whole system felt jagged and torn as she wondered what *really* made Keith Owens tick these days. Was she being too hard on him? What if all he wanted was a renewal of the wonderful friendship they had enjoyed from childhood to college? Goodness, true friendship was something to cherish, and wasn't it also a rarity? Could she honestly say that her current friends were more valuable, more precious than Keith had been for such a very long time?

You ninny! If all he wants is friendship he would not have kissed you in the limousine! Don't kid yourself about what he wants. You know full well what's on his lecherous mind! You didn't sleep with him in college, and he's determined to move you from the "Got Away" to the "Nailed Her" columns of his journal of sexual conquests.

Andrea jumped when Keith touched her shoulder and said, "All done, Teach. Here's your book." He grinned at her. "Where were you, off in fantasy land?"

"Yes," she said dryly. "It was definitely a fantasy." Rising, she left her desk and walked closer to the children. "It's time for recess. Everyone stand, please, and walk with me. Remember that we always leave quietly."

Keith followed them out and for the first time really observed Andrea and her class on the playground. She was so great with those kids, he thought, and it was obvious to him that they adored her. She never raised her voice to get them to do something, or to stop them from doing something. They obeyed her without whining, dragging their feet or questioning her request. She would be—Keith's breath caught over the thought—an incredible mother.

He left when the class went back inside the building, but waited in his car in the parking lot. Andrea saw him the second she came through the front door and she stopped on the stoop to assess the situation. Actually she only had two choices: continue their ridiculous squabbling, for which she blamed herself, for Keith had not said one insulting or demeaning thing to her while she had lambasted him at every opportunity, or be nice to him. After all, pleasantness toward a man certainly did not have to include anything sexual, and she was many years away from awkwardness around the opposite sex. Actually, it was Keith's misfortune to have suddenly developed silly ideas about her, not hers. She could handle Keith, she thought with a squaring of her shoulders, and he would eventually get the message that she wished he would return to the past and stay there.

Andrea walked directly to her car, but she didn't pretend that Keith wasn't there. Instead, she looked his way and said clearly, "You did a marvelous job with that story. The children enjoyed your rendition very much."

Pleased as punch with her compliment, Keith got out of his car and walked over to her. "Do you want to hear something funny? I enjoyed it, too. Andrea, I'm beginning to see why you were so set on becoming a teacher."

It was a sore subject for Andrea, because she would never forget how cruelly he had accused her of wasting her talents, her education and certainly her future by teaching instead of going into the computer software business with him. He couldn't have forgotten that awful night, any more than she did. But she'd decided on the school's stoop to be nice, and so she smiled and nodded and acted as though he hadn't just slammed her with a painful reminder of the past.

"Well, I really must be going," she said cordially. "I have a thousand things to do today." She got into her car.

Before she could close herself in, though, Keith took hold of the door and bent from the waist to peer into the car at her.

"Andrea, would you have dinner with me sometime?" he asked softly.

"Uh…dinner?" Damn it, she'd given an inch and now he wanted a mile! "Keith, really…I…I rarely go out."

"You're not known for being a run-around," he replied with an amused grin, "but I've seen you eating out with friends with my own eyes."

"Well, of course…on occasion," she said rather sharply. "But…I can't…I just can't…go out…with you."

Keith narrowed his eyes. He'd been thrilled with what she'd given him today, but it wasn't enough. He didn't let his disappointment show, though. "All right, maybe some other time," he said congenially, and stepped away from her car.

Keith didn't have to follow closely behind her because he knew the way to her house, and he could tell from the route she was driving that home was where she was going.

Andrea couldn't get rid of the tremor in the pit of her stomach. No matter how she treated Keith—disdainfully or pleasantly—he stayed one step ahead of her. She raised her garage door with her remote and drove in, relieved to be home and…and safe from Keith's magnetism.

"Nooo," she moaned. Keith's magnetism? What was wrong with her?

In the next instant she realized Keith's car was precisely behind hers! He'd followed her home. She stared in the rearview mirror as though she'd lost the mobility to do anything but sit right where she was.

Keith got out, quietly shut the door of his car and walked into her garage. Using the button on the wall, he dropped the garage door, and Andrea's pulse went wild. They were so alone, so completely isolated from everyone else in Royal. She wasn't sure she could keep him at arm's length any longer. In spite of old hurts, his infectious grin, his good looks and now his sweetness with the little darlings in her class were working some sort of magic on her.

Keith opened the door of her car and she didn't move a muscle, just sat there rigidly and stared straight ahead through the windshield.

"Andy?" he said quietly.

She still wouldn't look at him. "This is too much, Keith. Why are you here, invading my home, my space?"

"Please don't put it that way." But, of course, she'd only said the truth. He *was* invading her space and he suddenly wasn't so sure of himself. "I never seem to do anything right with you," he said with a deep frown between his eyes.

The pathos in his voice caused Andrea to finally look at him. "Why do you want to? I…don't understand you," she said in a shaky, husky voice.

"I don't understand you, either, but I want to. Andrea, would you and I becoming friends again be so terrible?"

''Friendship isn't the only thing on your mind.''

''That's true, but I'm willing to start there.'' He let a few moments of silence go by, then quietly asked, ''Could I see the inside of your house? You couldn't begin to know how many times I've driven past this pretty house and wondered what you were doing.''

''You haven't,'' she said, sounding totally deflated. ''Tell me you haven't been doing that.''

''Do you want me to lie?'' He held out his hand to help her from the car. ''Take me inside. Give me a glass of tea or a soda and talk to me. Treat me like an old friend, for that's what I am, Andy, what I'll always be no matter how determinedly you fight it.''

Andrea looked at that hand, his hand, and knew that if she took it and invited him in for a soda and conversation that she would be making a grave mistake. He was stronger-willed than she was, and gradually he was wearing her down.

But then she raised her eyes to gaze into his, and she felt sixteen again, about the time in her teen years when he had changed from her best buddy to the center of her universe. She knew now, of course, that he'd done nothing to cause her such a drastic change of heart. To him she'd still been best ''bud'' and the girl next door.

Looking into his gloriously alive brown eyes, every memory she possessed about him went sailing through her brain, leaving behind a star-sprinkled trail of emotions she had thought were dead and buried.

Apparently not. She reached out and took his hand. ''I'll fix some lunch for both of us,'' she said with a catch in her voice, knowing he'd won, that he'd negated her every objection and beaten her.

She could only hope now that he wouldn't make a pass because she'd never been so unsure of herself before. At least, not in a very long time.

Five

Keith liked Andrea's home the second he stepped inside. "It's nice, Andrea. Warm, very pleasant."

"Thank you. Look around, if you wish. I'll be in the kitchen."

"Thanks, I will."

When he strolled away she physically wilted against the refrigerator. It didn't seem possible that Keith was actually there, in her house. And not for a social gathering of friends and acquaintances, but alone, by himself!

Andrea quietly groaned. Her heart seemed to be fluttering nervously, as were her stomach and hands. Why had she let herself be drawn into this situation? She could have stood her ground in the garage and told him to leave her property at once. But no, she'd caved in and invited him to lunch!

Lunch. What on earth was she going to feed him? Quickly she turned and opened the door of the refrigerator. Scanning the shelves, she added up what she had on hand. Fine, she thought, and went to the sink to wash her hands. Returning to the refrigerator, she began taking out ingredients.

Keith came back while she was setting the table. They would eat in the kitchen's dining nook rather than in her formal dining room. Not that she wanted things cozy between them, but a spur-of-the-moment luncheon should be casually prepared and served.

"Can I help?" he asked.

"Everything's taken care of." Andrea walked from the nook to the counter, where she began putting the finishing touches to a bowl of chicken salad. "Have a seat," she said without looking at him.

Keith wandered over to the counter with its three stools and sat on one. "Do you remember when we were kids and you would go into your house, make a pile of peanut butter and jelly sandwiches and bring them outside to our fort?"

"Along with as many cartons of juice I could carry."

"You haven't forgotten our fort, then."

"Of course not. It was a big part of my childhood."

"Mine, too. One day it would be a spaceship and the next a rustler's hideout. We had great imaginations back then, Andy."

"Most children do." She wanted to ask him to please stick with her given name, and not to shorten it or alter it, but she refrained from doing so.

"Too bad we all have to grow up," Keith murmured. "It happens so fast."

"When childhood is thirty years ago, it seems that it flew by much too quickly. We never truly enjoy each and every phase of life until it's gone. I let my teens and then my twenties rush by without ever stopping my hectic pace long enough to relish any one particular age."

"I know what you mean. Now we're both eight years into our thirties. Are you still letting a hectic pace rule your heart?"

Andrea felt her cheeks turn pink. She'd said nothing at all

about her heart, and she was not going to be led down *that* path!

"Are you?" she asked, throwing him a challenging glance.

Keith smiled teasingly. "I asked you first."

"You used to pull that on me when we were kids, if I remember correctly," she said and gave her chicken salad a final stir. "Lunch is ready," she announced. "Please bring that pitcher of iced tea to the table."

When they were seated and eating, Keith began another conversation. "Do you ever feel old?"

Startled, Andrea lowered her fork. "I'm not sure that's a question I care to answer."

"You don't look much older than you did in college, you know, but you could dress younger."

"And what's wrong with this dress?" It was a pretty dress, pink cotton with white trim.

"Its style is too old for you."

"Good Lord, Keith, I'm a teacher! Should I wear short skirts and halter tops to teach youngsters?"

"I guess not, but do you even *own* a short skirt and a halter top?"

"That's none of your business," she grumbled. "Look, you worry about your wardrobe and I'll worry about mine."

"Sorry. Obviously I hit a nerve."

"You have no right even to comment on my clothing, let alone judge and censure it."

"Don't get all steamed up. You always look nice, whatever you're wearing."

"Then why say something as rude as that remark about my dressing younger?"

"I apologize again. You looked great at the ball."

"Young enough for your juvenile taste?" she drawled.

"You're all fired up and sarcastic. I take it back, okay? Anything I said that might have annoyed you, I take it back."

"You should."

"I do, but it wouldn't hurt you to answer my question."

"What question?"

"Do you ever feel old? I guess I'm asking because every so often I feel older than my dad was when he passed away. He was sixty. Mother was sixty-two when she died."

"About the same ages as my parents were when they died," Andrea said quietly. "They all died too young. I have friends well into their seventies and eighties who are active and great fun to be with. Of course, they're in reasonably good health, which makes a major difference, but I also think a sense of humor helps to keep people young."

"Could be. You used to have a great sense of humor."

"Meaning I don't now?"

"Now don't go getting all puffed up again. All I said was…"

"I know what you said."

"Well, how would I know if you still love to laugh when we rarely see each other? Andrea, when you really think about it, isn't it silly for you and I to be anything but the closest of friends?"

Instantly wary, Andrea covered her fluster by picking up the pitcher of tea and refilling their glasses. She had to say something, give him some kind of reply, but what?

She finally said, rather stiffly, "It's not so silly, Keith. We didn't part on the best of terms, you know."

"But that was a hundred years ago! Andy, I have so many feelings for you. What should I do with them?"

"They're all *old* feelings, Keith, part of the past! Leave them there."

"Sometimes old things are the best. Can new friends really replace old ones? I don't think so. Andy, I'm lonely."

Her jaw dropped. "Now, *that's* a lie!"

"No, sweetheart, it isn't. Yes, I have friends, lots of them, and I've got money and community respect. But there's a hole right about here…" He laid his hand on his abdomen. "…that I can't seem to fill."

"Have some more chicken salad," she said dryly, giving him a glib answer. What a con artist!

Keith couldn't help laughing. "Well, I can see that your

sense of humor is still alive and thriving. That's good.'' After a few silent moments he said, "But I wasn't lying about being lonely.''

"Maybe not, but why tell me about it? Every adult in the world who lives alone probably has moments of loneliness. It's hardly a fatal affliction."

"You're thinking that I'm looking for sympathy."

"You are," she said flatly. "But you're looking in the wrong place, and from the wrong person."

"I never dreamed you could be so cold."

"If a realistic take on life translates to a cold attitude to you, there's not much I can do about it."

"You're not cold with the kids in your class." Keith put his elbows on the table and leaned forward to look directly into her eyes. "You're magnificent with those children, and it's obvious as anything I've ever seen that they adore you. You love them, don't you? You pour all your emotion like a stream of liquid gold into that one glorious outlet, and you can do it day after day, month after month because it's safe. There's not a sliver of danger from loving children, is there? Nothing at all like what can happen if you let yourself love a grown-up."

Andrea refused to look away from the smug expression on his face. In a way it amused her that he actually believed that he'd figured her out so easily, but there *was* a grain of truth in his analysis. The "safety" factor he'd mentioned wasn't entirely incorrect, but neither was it accurate. Should she set him straight on that or let him wallow in his misconceptions?

"If you're expecting me to debate with you over my affection for young children, you're going to be sadly disappointed."

"Then everything I said must be true."

Andrea shrugged. "Think so if you wish. I don't owe you anything, Keith, least of all an explanation of why I behave as I do. The truth is, I don't owe anything to anyone and I like it that way."

Keith narrowed his eyes on her. "In other words, you're *never* lonely."

"We're back to that? Sorry, but that bait still isn't going to work."

"Bait?"

"You're fishing, Keith. What you're hoping to unearth from deep within my psyche is beyond me, but you've got something in mind."

He leaned back in his chair and regarded her solemnly. "I already explained it. I want us to be friends."

She was suddenly furious. "*Kissing* friends?" she spat. "We might have stood a chance if you hadn't made that insulting pass the night of the ball. What did you think I was going to do, fall into your arms like some...some sex-starved tart?"

"It was only a kiss, Andy. You really didn't hate it that much, did you?"

"It was a shock that I hope will never be repeated." Pushing back her chair, Andrea got up and began clearing the table.

Keith rose to help. Carrying dishes, cutlery and leftover food they passed each other twice before everything was on the counter and Andrea could wipe down the table. Andrea's mind wished Keith would say "Thanks, goodbye," and leave, but there was a different tune playing elsewhere in her body. She didn't want the feelings there, she *hated* the tingles and flutterings of her own female system caused by a man that intellectually she wanted no part of.

Such feelings were confusing her to the point that she wasn't sure of what to do next. Considering her "marvelous hostess" reputation, she was behaving out of character. Her friends would not have recognized the woman she was today, for none of them had ever seen this uncertain side of her. Keith had. She hadn't always been resolute and confident. She'd been soft in her youth, starry-eyed over anything that smacked of romance. She'd seen love where there'd been none. The partnership *Keith* had been thinking about had been all business. She might as well have been his cousin.

Why didn't he leave? He'd had his lunch and his say, and it was all he was going to get from her. Should she come right out and ask him to leave?

She tried to ignore his watchful gaze as she rinsed the lunch dishes and put them in the dishwasher. "Did you see the backyard?" she asked, striving for a casualness she was far from feeling.

"Only through the windows. Your yard is beautiful."

"I designed it."

"The pool, too?"

"All of it. When I bought this house it was extremely plain. It had this great floor plan and it was exactly the size home I was looking for, but the former owners had done very little to it in the way of interior décor and exterior landscaping. The entire yard was grass and a few trees, and since I intended to live my life here, I wanted everything perfect. Perfect for me, that is."

"You did a good job."

"I think so. I'm sure the whole house would fit in the foyer of yours, but..."

"Totally irrelevant," Keith said before she'd finished speaking. "Why didn't you stay in the house that you lived in during your marriage?"

Andrea stiffened. "I didn't want to," she said sharply.

"That's no answer. Your leaving that house for this one makes me wonder: you didn't love Jerry O'Rourke, did you?"

She gasped out loud and swung around to face him. "I most certainly did love Jerry! What gives you the right to even mention my marriage? I had a good marriage and I was happy. I will never get over losing Jerry."

"If that's all true, then I owe you an apology. Thing is, Andy darlin', it sounds more like a fairy tale than the truth."

"Why?" she demanded angrily. "Because *your* marriage was such a bust?"

"Maybe," he said, sounding speculative. "One question springs to mind, doesn't it? Am I petty enough to doubt your happy marriage because mine wasn't?"

"And how could the great Keith Owens *ever* acknowledge something so human as pettiness, right?"

"Well, the idea does sort of pinch," he replied with a grin.

"You're impossible."

"I've heard that before, so you could be right."

Andrea closed the door of the dishwasher, rinsed her hands at the sink and dried them with a paper towel.

"You're the only man I know who's proud of his faults," she said with a scorching look at him.

"You're beautiful when your fire's up and burning," he told her.

"*Nothing's* burning. Nothing's even warm, so don't waste your breath, Keith." She realized that he'd taken two steps toward her, and she backed up. "If you try anything I swear I'll brain you with a skillet!"

"No, you won't." He advanced farther, and she found her backside against the counter. "Tell me you don't feel anything," he said in a low, husky voice that alarmed her more than his proximity.

"This is the reason you followed me home, isn't it?" she said accusingly. "Not to reestablish friendship but to make another pass. Well, maybe we should just go to bed and get it over with. Once should be enough, don't you think?"

He was so stunned he couldn't say a word for a very long moment. Finally he cleared his throat and managed a hoarse, "You never used to talk like that."

"I could talk plainer," she snapped. "You're not irresistible, Keith. I live alone because I want to. I do not want another man, another husband. I'm without a man by choice! Do you get my drift? If I've been too subtle, say so and I'll draw you a picture!"

Keith held up his hands in total surrender. "You win. I won't try to kiss you again, though I'd like you to remember that kissing you and making love to you are the uppermost thoughts in my mind every time I'm near you.''

Andrea stared. "You're planning to be near me again?"

"Every chance I get, darlin', every chance I get. Thank you for lunch and I enjoyed our conversation, before I went and ruined everything by behaving like a man who admires a woman more than he can express in mere words. That's when the need for kissing and all that other stuff overwhelms one's good sense. I won't be at the preschool tomorrow because I have a meeting, but I will be seeing you again very soon.''

He walked out of Andrea's kitchen, whistling a merry tune. She stared after him like a sleepwalker, dazed both in eye and spirit. No matter how she treated him, no matter what she said or did, he always seemed to get the last word. How could he always stay one step ahead of her?

But the worst, most painful, question to ponder was why she had relented so drastically and actually invited him into her home. Something told her there was no eradicating what she'd done today. He had a foothold now, and *she'd given it to him!*

"My God, why?" she whispered.

The rest of the day was a bust for Andrea. There were a dozen things she could—and probably should—have done, but she couldn't seem to get herself together enough to accomplish anything constructive. After Keith left she had donned yard clothes and forced herself outside to search the beds of flowers for weeds. The man she employed for yard work did an excellent job, and he didn't need her to keep the flowers and grass free of weeds.

And so she sat in the shade on the patio, gazed upon her beautiful backyard and brooded over Keith. It was awful to feel so helpless about something, for she *wasn't* helpless. Not ordinarily, anyway. But this…this invasion of her privacy, of her personal life, had her frustrated and stymied.

Hoping to relieve her mind of anything remotely connected

to Keith, she deliberately thought of the people she paid to keep her home in A1 condition. There was Lucyanne, the lady who came to the house once a week and made the whole place shine and smell good from aromatic cleaning products and elbow grease. Hector came twice a week to clean the pool and check the chemical balance of the water, and finally there was Jake, whom she rarely saw because he kindly co-incided his lawn-mowing with her morning classes at Kiddie Kingdom.

She had it good and knew it. Or she *had* known it, believed it with all her heart, but now, watching the sun creating silver streaks in the aquamarine water of her pool, there was a rest-lessness within her that she couldn't seem to dent. Well, yes, her loyal household helpers were blessings, and so were her friends and her job and the investments inherited from her parents and from Jerry. Everything she had was a blessing, for there were so many people with so very little in the way of material comfort. She understood that very well, thanked her lucky stars and was more than generous with donations to worthy charities. Plus, of course, she gave more than money to New Hope, she gave some of herself—her time, perhaps the most intrinsically valuable donation of all.

Andrea heaved a long-drawn-out sigh and blamed Keith for causing her such an awful case of the blues. She'd been hard on him and in a way she was sorry, mostly because she wasn't normally unkind to anyone. But Keith scared her. He was a disruption in every way possible. She'd been com-pletely contented before the Cattleman's Club ball and now she wasn't, and who or what else *should* she blame for that? No, Keith was definitely the cause of her discontentment, and by his own words, he was not going to leave her alone.

How to deal with this? How to deal with an unwanted Romeo? The questions went around and around in her mind. If someone had noticed Keith's dark-blue SUV in her drive-way today—and it seemed pretty farfetched to assume that no one had noticed it—then it was probably all over town by now that he'd been to her house.

"Who cares?" she mumbled. There were those in the area who never forgot anything, so a lot of Royal residents remembered that she and Keith had once been an item. A fresh new rumor might titillate imaginations for a while, but so what?

Sighing again, Andrea realized the afternoon was practically gone. She'd wasted hours brooding over Keith's brazenness. Whenever Keith had wanted something, even as a child, he'd gone after it like a hound on the scent of a rabbit.

Well, in this case, she, apparently, was the rabbit!

"Damn you, Keith," she muttered and got up from her patio chair and went inside.

On Friday, Keith did not come to her classroom. He'd told her he wouldn't be there, but Andrea really didn't believe anything he said. Oddly, that empty little chair at the back of the room bothered her in some unfathomable way, because she found herself looking at it far too often.

It also bothered some of the children, whom Andrea saw glancing toward the back of the room several times. For the first time since she'd begun teaching at Kiddie Kingdom, she was glad when school was out for the day and she could go home. Telling herself it was only because she had so many things to do to prepare for her dinner party that evening, she drove from the school to her favorite supermarket.

That afternoon she accomplished a great deal. With five good friends coming for dinner, she couldn't just sit around and worry today. She shopped, she drove home with a back seat full of groceries, she cooked and she tried almost desperately to lock Keith out of her thoughts.

By six-thirty the dinner menu was ready except for a few final touches that could only be done just before serving, Andrea was dressed in a lovely hostess gown the same color as her eyes, and, of course, thanks to Lucyanne, the house was perfect. To the spotlessly clean rooms, Andrea had added numerous vases of freshly cut flowers. She loved candles, but omitted them this evening because one of her guests was allergic to the smoke.

Ten minutes before seven her guests began arriving. Everyone there knew Andrea's routine. Cocktails at seven, dinner at seven-thirty. She poured herself a glass of wine and joined her friends already involved in a rather humorous dissection of a recent bestselling book. Andrea wasn't quite through reading it, but when she stated rather flatly that she didn't like the book and probably *wouldn't* finish it, five sets of eyes looked at her in surprise.

Then the arguments began. Her friends were going to convince her that the book might have flaws, but wasn't it possible the author deliberately included them to make readers think?

For the first time ever Andrea didn't give a whit about the friendly, rapid-fire debate. Realizing that startled her, for she had always loved intellectual debates with these wonderful friends. She excused herself on a kitchen-duty pretext and fled the room.

Breathing hard, as though she'd just run her usual three miles, she strode through the kitchen and went outside through the garage. Standing in the shadows of garage and house, she breathed in the cool night air and tried to pull herself together. Nothing was the same as it had been before the Cattleman's Club ball, and she had the most awful urge just to let go and cry her eyes out.

Which she couldn't do. She had to return to her guests. She had to smile and talk and act as though her life was the same smooth and serene routine it had been for years. She had to serve her marvelous dinner and talk again while everyone ate it. And then she had to offer after-dinner drinks, which everyone would accept, and talk again. For hours. At least until eleven, although some of her dinner parties had run past midnight.

She was just turning to go back inside when she heard a car on her street. It was moving slowly and when she looked she saw that it was a dark SUV. That was Keith's SUV, she'd bet her life on it! Now he was driving past her house at night? What next?

Keith saw the cars in Andrea's driveway. She had guests. He turned at the end of her street and drove home.

When he got there he turned on Eric's computer once again and opened the numeric file he'd found. Studying the rows of unbroken double-spaced numbers, which made absolutely no sense, as every type of written record contained vacant spaces, he began playing around, trying various tests, such as eliminating certain numbers or combinations of numbers.

He worked for several hours, accomplished nothing concrete or conclusive, and finally went to bed. The second his head hit the pillow there wasn't a number anywhere in his brain. In fact the only thing occupying that particular part of his anatomy was an image of Andrea's face. And she wasn't looking at him with a kindly expression, either.

Grunting in frustration, he punched his pillow.

Six

Andrea bid her guests good-night with her usual warm, winning smile. They complimented her delicious dinner and exemplary hospitality and departed in high spirits shortly before eleven. Relieved that no one seemed to have picked up on her jittery mood, Andrea busied herself picking up glasses from various tables in the living room and carrying them to the kitchen.

She went to her bedroom then to change into her nightgown and summer-weight robe, for comfort mostly, but also to avoid the risk of spilling or splashing something onto the exquisite fabric of her blue dress, and returned to the kitchen.

All the while her mind jumped from one thing to another, mostly from her established routine to Keith, who had disrupted longtime habits and rituals. She resented him terribly. If he stayed on his side of Pine Valley, she wouldn't have to resent him at all. She would hardly be aware of his existence, which was precisely how their non-relationship had flowed

along—with only an occasional discomfiting lurch—for years
and years.

But he did what he wanted. He always had, if she looked
back and recalled the bossy, mouthy little boy he'd been,
even though he'd also been her best friend. And then, at
thirty-eight years old, from out of the blue, some weird event
had made him see her in a brand-new way. And he had the
bloody gall to think she should be thrilled about it! What
exactly could she do about such arrogance?

She was still deep in thought on the subject when her front
doorbell chimed, startling her so much that she nearly
dropped the plate in her hand. Quickly gathering her wits—
a guest must have accidentally left something behind—she
dried her hands and hurried to the foyer.

Switching on the outside light, which she'd turned off once
her dinner guests had driven away, she peered through the
peephole in the door. Her jaw dropped, her stomach knotted
and her pulse began racing: It was Keith!

The bell chimed again. Drawing a huge breath, Andrea
unlocked and opened the door a crack. "It's late. Why are
you here?"

"I saw your lights. May I come in?"

"What for?"

"Because I need a friend."

"Oh, you're in one of your lonely moods." She knew she
sounded cruel, and she really didn't want to hurt Keith. But
who else did she know who would ring her doorbell at this
time of night? *Her* friends were considerate. *Her* friends
called before dropping in.

Keith slapped at a moth that had been drawn by the light.
"To be perfectly honest, I thought about what you said yesterday, and I think you just might be right."

"What did I say?"

Another moth buzzed Keith's head and he made a swipe
at it. "Could I please come inside and escape these critters?"

Grudgingly she opened the door and stepped back so he

could enter. "What did I say yesterday?" she repeated stonily.

"Hey, do I smell coffee? Would it be too much trouble to give me a cup?"

She shook her head disgustedly. "You have more bullish brass than Texas longhorns. If you want some coffee it's in the kitchen." Spinning on her heel, she walked away.

Grinning all over his face, positive that she wasn't really angry with him for dropping in uninvited but she had to act that way, he stayed right behind her. "How'd your party go? Ended kind of early, didn't it? What happened? Wasn't it any fun? Did you make the mistake of inviting a bunch of boring people over?"

She swung around to face him. "My friends are not boring! We had a perfectly lovely evening."

"A lovely evening that stopped dead before the clock struck eleven, let alone twelve?"

"I suppose *your* parties are just beginning at eleven, probably with every guest falling down drunk by twelve! Well, my friends don't happen to enjoy that sort of sport, old *sport!*"

He reached out and gently brushed a strand of hair from her cheek, shocking her to immobility, and said softly, "How come I rile you so much, sweetheart?"

Andrea swallowed hard and forced her feet to step away from him. Going to the coffeemaker, she filled a cup and then brought it to the counter. "Sugar, cream?" she asked in a voice she barely recognized as her own. He changed who she normally was, she thought unhappily. That was his secret, his power; he had the ability to eradicate all the gentility she'd acquired through the years and leave her with nothing but a raw inner core.

"Black, just the way it is." Keith sat on a counter stool and lifted the cup to his lips for a sip, keeping his eyes on her all the while. Her robe had not been designed for seduction, but it seduced him, probably because it *was* a robe, which hinted at a flimsy gown and nothing else under it.

"Was your party a shower of some sort?" he asked.

"A shower! Why on earth would you think that?"

"Because of your robe."

It took a second for her to make the connection between *shower* and *robe,* and when she did she couldn't help smiling.

"You're incorrigible," she said.

Keith smiled at her. "Have some coffee with me."

"Might as well," she muttered, totally giving up on ever besting him. "I already knew I wasn't going to get much sleep tonight."

"Why not, hon?"

His endearment caused a shiver to travel her spine. Holding her cup of coffee in front of her, she hit him with a hard look. "You know damned well why not."

"Not because of anything I've done. Maybe because your party was a bust?"

"It was *not* a bust! Damn, you're irritating."

"Did you just now come to that conclusion?"

"Hardly."

"Well, if I'm so irritating and you thought so before now, how come you let me in?"

"Yes, let's get back to that. What did I say yesterday that you decided was so agreeable that you had to come by in the middle of the night to remind me of it? And I would appreciate a straightforward answer, if you don't mind."

Keith slowly took another swallow of coffee and tested her patience further by narrowing his eyes as though deep in thought.

"Will you please get to it?" she demanded hotly.

"Well, on second thought maybe I shouldn't."

"Oh, for crying out loud!"

"You might get upset."

"I'm *already* upset!"

"Yeah, I guess you are. I upset you pretty easily, don't I?"

"I don't have words to describe *how* easily."

He ignored her sarcasm and mused aloud, "I wonder why that is."

The red-hot anger rising within her wasn't a pleasant sensation, and she was honestly afraid of where it might lead. She gritted her teeth and forced herself to speak normally.

"I don't have to wonder, I know. Now, take this any way you wish, but either tell me what I said yesterday that intrigued you so...the *only* reason I opened my door to you at this hour...or leave. Those are your choices."

"Okay, but remember you insisted on candor. You said that we should probably go to bed together and get it out of our systems. I'd like to take you up on that offer."

Andrea slumped against the refrigerator and just stared at him. "You're insane."

"Did you or did you not say those very words?"

"Not in the context you're construing them!"

"Oh. Well, what other meaning could an invitation to join you in bed have?"

"I didn't invite you to join me in bed!" she shrieked. "That is not what I said!"

"I'm afraid it is, Andy," he said with a smile she would just love to smear across his face with a hard slap.

"Leave!" she shouted. "Get your butt off that stool and leave my house!"

"Well, if you're going to get all bent out of shape over some simple conversation, then fine, I'll be happy to go." Keith set down his cup and got off the stool.

Andrea was breathing hard, so full of righteous fury that her color was high and her bosom heaving. There was also discomfort in her chest, not a piercing physical pain that would frighten a person, but a thudding ache without a name. It was there, and she knew nothing about its cause or meaning, other than it was somehow connected to Keith. Or maybe it was a reminder of Keith, perhaps a ball of memories that had wound around itself so tightly for so many years in her effort to forget all that had been good between them that it was now wizened and almost unrecognizable.

Then, with a swiftness and strength that took her breath, some part of herself that was alien to the woman she'd been for a very long time urged her to find her voice and call him back, to ask him to stay and finish his coffee. Surely they could talk without anger, couldn't they? She opened her mouth, but nothing came out of it.

Keith walked around the counter and started to leave the kitchen, but then he took her completely by surprise and reversed direction in a fast-moving blur. Her back still to the refrigerator, he pinned her with his body pressed against hers and looked deeply into her shell-shocked eyes.

"You're a beauty, Andy," he said huskily. "You clearly said that we should go to bed together, and I did *not* misinterpret your meaning. You were thinking that we stir each other's emotions far too much to pretend we're unaware of it, and that maybe it was because we never really made love when we should have. You were hoping, I think, that one time together would kill the bad case of nerves we have around each other. You could be right, although I'm not positive of that. One time together might only open a dam of desire that neither of us could even imagine. But I'm willing to take that chance, if you are."

"I...didn't mean it the way you...took it."

"Oh?"

"I think I was...uh, trying to get across to you a completely different kind of...message." Truthfully she couldn't remember why she'd said something so unbelievably stupid. She should have known how he would take it. And she was still reacting stupidly to him, thinking that the ache in her chest could be a bunch of old memories that refused to stay buried.

But she had another, more urgent concern at the moment, an unfamiliar physical weakness. Her muscles felt rubbery and all but useless, her legs threatening to buckle, and if he wasn't pressed so tightly against her, she was quite certain that she would slide down the face of the refrigerator like a wave of hot liquid.

Nervously she licked her lips. Whatever else she did or didn't know, one thing was clear: she had to break this up and get him out of her house.

"You...I..." Stumbling over simple words was foreign and embarrassing, and she felt impossibly adolescent.

"What, sweetheart? Say it." Keith lowered his head so his lips were but a breath from hers. "Tell me what you want," he whispered.

What you want...what you want. The words repeated in her bewildered brain, for what she wanted was something she *hadn't* wanted in years. Even more painful to contemplate was why she would feel all silky and sensual now because of a man she didn't even like. She wished she weren't thinking such things.

Only now she couldn't push the tantalizing topic from her mind. Keith's body was hard and yet yielded to her female curves. She was dazed and yearning, aching in places that had felt nothing for so long.

So, what did she want? Her heart could have said the words if it could speak, but the part of her that *could* speak, her mouth, simply would not cooperate.

"I...I want you to leave," she said and stunned herself by sounding like a rusty spring.

Keith's dark eyes were traveling her face with a smoldering light. "And I want you," he said in a low-pitched, gravelly voice. "How are we going to align our differing desires?"

"We...we aren't," she whispered. "We...can't. We..." It was the last word she said before his lips settled on hers. A moan rose in her throat as her body caught fire. His nervy connecting of their bodies, his nearness, that low, bedroom voice in which he'd been speaking had all been foreplay, and it had worked. She slid her hands up his chest, locked them together behind his head and opened her mouth to suck on his tongue. Oh, what joy, she thought dizzily. *Why* had she relegated these incredible feelings to the trash bin after

Jerry's death? Other widows grieved and then lived again. Why hadn't she?

She wriggled herself closer to Keith and kissed him with a rare, ravenous hunger. Her feverish passion startled Keith so much that he broke the kiss and tilted his head back to scrutinize the features of her face. Was this real? He'd been hoping to arouse her, but had he really believed in his ability to do so? Something didn't feel quite right, though for the life of him he couldn't figure out what it might be. Andrea had never kissed him like this when they were both young and randy in college. Something was *very* odd here.

It struck him then that he could have her tonight, right now, in her own kitchen or wherever he chose. If ever a woman was ripe and lushly ready for lovemaking, it was Andrea, and it just didn't add up. Running hot and cold was one thing, but this was...well, it was astounding. Keith's heart sank. Something told him to get the hell out of there, and it seemed so ludicrous when this was what he'd been wanting from Andrea. But he couldn't take this to the next level. Not tonight, he couldn't.

He slid her arms from around his neck, kissed her lips lightly and said, "You were right, it's late. May I call you tomorrow?"

She was almost too thunderstruck to speak. Why had he stopped? She didn't want him to stop!

"Yes...I suppose," she mumbled.

"Good night. Sleep well." Keith walked out of the kitchen and in a few seconds she heard the front door open and close. What had just happened? she asked herself. Dazed and confused, she stumbled to a chair and fell into it. She sat there numbly and tried to find some sense in Keith's visit.

She couldn't do it. There was no sense to it, certainly none in the way he'd talked about making love and then kissed her the way he had, only to back off when she kissed back.

Strangely, though, when she finally went to bed and stared at the darkened ceiling, her thoughts were more on herself than on Keith's peculiar behavior. In fact, her own behavior was far more peculiar than his, and it made her cry to think about it.

She finally fell asleep with wet, teary eyes and a heavy heart.

Keith didn't go straight home from Andrea's house. Instead, he drove to the Cattleman's Club, parked and turned off the engine of his SUV. There were times when the club was more welcoming than his own home, and he started to get out to go inside when he spotted vehicles belonging to friends parked in the lot. They would call him over, ask him to join them, and those that knew him best would see that something was wrong and, with all good intentions, even ask him about his downcast demeanor.

And what would he say? You're looking at a fool. I had her in the palm of my hand and I walked away.

Heaving a sigh, he decided against going in but he didn't immediately restart the motor and leave. He sat behind the wheel staring through the windshield at nothing in particular, remembering that kiss and wondering…wondering with every cell in his body. Surely Andrea's response hadn't scared him off. No, he hadn't been scared. He'd been stunned, but why, for God's sake? Why wouldn't she be more passionate now? She'd been married, she was a mature woman and everyone learned and changed with time.

But as logical as that explanation was, it didn't sit right. The problem hadn't been Andrea's response, it had been his! How could he be so damned ambiguous about something he'd been so positive of wanting? He *still* wanted her! Didn't he?

Sighing, Keith tried and couldn't put it all together, the old memories—so many of them pure gold—with Andrea's consistently distant treatment of him since college, and now this. Why in heaven's name hadn't he stayed? Not just to make love, but to talk. To *really* talk. Damn, instead of confronting her ardent mood he'd run away like a schoolboy, red-faced after his first kiss.

He finally drove home, disgusted with himself and wondering who the real Andrea was these days.

Andrea began her early-morning run on Saturday with none of her normal exuberance. She felt listless, in fact, and hoped that some extra oxygen in her blood from physical exertion would bring her back to life. She always spent time at New Hope on Saturdays, and she didn't want to go in looking like the last rose of summer.

It was how she felt, though, and she only got as far as Royal Park when her willpower totally deserted her. Stumbling to one of the benches near the lake, she collapsed on it. In seconds, tears began filling her eyes, a humiliation in public. But it was very early and while there were some other early birds in the park, no one was close enough to see Andrea O'Rourke crying without a sound, just sitting there while tears dribbled down her cheeks.

She angrily dashed them away. There was something wrong with her, and she fully intended to find out what it was. Kissing Keith the way she had last night and then being turned down was more humiliating than crying in the park, for heaven's sake.

"Oh, stop it," she muttered and got up from the bench and ran for home.

Andrea put in her time at New Hope that day, but though she tried not to be impatient to be out of there, she couldn't enjoy her hours at the charity facility as she usually did. Perhaps *enjoyment* wasn't the right word to describe her work with New Hope, for every woman seeking shelter and protection there had a sad and sometimes brutal story to tell. But helping people who truly needed it had been giving Andrea a satisfying sense of purpose. Today, while not proud of it, she was more concerned with herself than anyone in the shelter.

Finally she was able to leave, and she drove home wishing she could shake her dark and gloomy mood. When she got home, she sat at her small, elegant desk in her den, checked her voice mail and listened to messages from last night's guests thanking her. Courtesy was a high priority with her friends, and the additional thanks were no surprise.

Neither was Keith's voice in her ear. "Andy, you said it was all right to phone today, so that's what I'm doing. Sorry I missed you, but maybe you'll call me back. My number is 555-2777. I'd like us to get together. We could have dinner out or simply meet at your house or mine for some conversation. Anywhere is fine with me, so name it if you have a preference. I'd just like to see you. Uh, guess that's it. Call me, please."

Andrea put down the phone and then sat numbly. For her, the day had been emotionally painful. She'd teetered all day on the very edge of a really powerful crying spell, and would seeing Keith again so soon change that? She found it hard to believe that it might.

Why was this happening to her? She hadn't found celibacy trying before this, probably because no other man had moved her in the way Keith had last night. Also, she really hadn't given any other man an opportunity to move her. Keith Owens had brought that obviously ignored and hidden side of herself into the sun, and why? How? Why him?

Why *not* him? she thought woefully. He *had* been her first love, after all.

Only she'd really known nothing at all about love at the time...certainly nothing of the physical side of love in college. All her fault, of course. She'd been so determined to be a virgin on her wedding night that she'd probably driven Keith away.

You most certainly did not drive him away! He did that himself by offering you a business proposition instead of offering you an engagement ring!

Yes, she'd been embarrassingly naive, but that had been a long time ago. She *hadn't* been even slightly naive last night and he'd walked away from her! Dammit, after all the chasing after her he'd done lately, she had a right to know why.

Reaching for the phone, she punched out Keith's number. He answered on the third ring.

"Hello," she replied to his greeting. "This is Andrea. I'm returning your call, and this may surprise you but I would like to get together this evening."

"This evening?" Keith echoed in surprise.

"Oh, didn't you mean tonight?"

"Yes…uh, yes! Tonight is great. Would you like to have dinner out?"

"No, I don't think so. Let's meet somewhere after dinner." She realized that she wasn't especially keen about his SUV showing up in her driveway again tonight, even though she really didn't care what the neighbors might think. But Keith was so well known in Royal, and deliberately inviting gossip didn't seem sensible, either. "How about…" She searched her mind for a place of privacy.

"Come to my house," Keith said brusquely. "I'll leave one of the garage doors open and you can park inside. No one will ever know you fell off the wagon and actually went to see a man."

She gasped. "Must you be so crude?"

"I was just beginning to believe that we both finally grew up," he retorted.

"Keith, I don't understand what's going on with us. Does that make me immature? I thought maybe if we did some talking…well, that's the reason I called. I…I'm not sure I know myself anymore and I sure as the devil don't know the man you are now."

"So all tonight is to you is a means to pick my brain. Okay, fine, I can live with that. I've been thinking we should do some talking anyhow. Maybe I don't know you anymore, either, and I want to, Andy, I want to know you in every way possible. What time should I expect you?"

After his statement of wanting to know her in every way possible she wondered if she shouldn't just cancel the whole thing. But she couldn't let sleeping dogs lie, not about this. He had finally succeeded in opening her eyes to the past, to the boy he'd been, the young man, to the many wonderful old memories she'd tried to bury, and he was *not* walking out of her life again as easily as he'd done in college.

"Around nine," she said flatly. "No, make it ten."

"After dark, huh?"

"Did you think I would deny it?"

"Andy, my sweet, I don't know *what* to think about anything you might say or do these days. But I'd like to. See you at ten."

Seven

Andrea paced and worried. Going to Keith's home bothered her. She wasn't ready for that step and should have thought the whole bizarre thing through better and had a specific meeting place in mind before calling him.

Irritated at her own reckless haste, she made a decision and dialed Keith's number again. When he answered she came right to the point.

"Andrea here. Are you free now?"

Keith was taken aback. "I'm hot and sweaty from working out in my home gym, but sure, I'm free. Well, maybe not free. You know the old joke. I might not be free, but I'm cheap."

"Yes," she said dryly. "I know the old joke. It doesn't apply, Keith. Not to me and not to you. We each come with loads of baggage."

"Meaning?"

"Thirty-eight years of baggage needs explanation?"

"Oh, I see what you mean. Okay, what's the pitch?"

"I've changed my mind about coming to your house and concealing my car in your garage. Lurking around in the shadows seems a bit too melodramatic. Anyhow, if you have the time now, I'd like us to meet in the park."

"Any particular place in the park?" he asked in his most pronounced Texas drawl, his way of letting someone know that he thought they just might be an egg or two short of a full dozen. Truth was, Andrea kept surprising him, and while some of her surprises were great, some were pretty far out and tough to swallow.

"Are you making fun of me?"

"Wouldn't dream of it. Where do you want to meet? It'll take me about twenty minutes to shower and make the drive."

"I intend to walk, so twenty minutes should be just about right. You remember where the old cannon is, don't you?"

"I know where it is, yes."

"Well, that's where I'll be."

"Fine. See you in a few."

Andrea hung up, then hurried to her bedroom to change into slacks and walking shoes. In minutes she was leaving the house and heading for the park. It was a glorious evening. Night was just beginning to fall, and the darkening of the sky combined with a spectacular sunset created a golden twilight. Hurrying along, she said hello to the people she encountered in her neighborhood without stopping to chat. An evening like this got folks outside, and she began worrying about how populated the park might be.

When she reached Royal Park, she relaxed considerably. There were people, quite a few of them, but no one was close to the old cannon, which resided on a square of cement and bore a bronze plaque honoring the bravery and patriotism of Texas men and women. Someone kept both the cannon and plaque polished, which always pleased Andrea although her thoughts were not on that small pleasure this evening.

She was on pins and needles, actually, anxious to talk to Keith and yet apprehensive. The truth was, now that she was here, what exactly was she so adamant about discussing with Keith? His college attitude? Hers? Good Lord, no.

Several benches faced the cannon, and Andrea chose one. She couldn't see the parking area from where she sat, which made watching for Keith rather difficult. She waited, grew impatient, checked her watch and waited some more. He was late.

Becoming more annoyed with his inconsiderate tardiness by the minute, she realized that people, especially those with small children, were leaving as darkness encroached on the lovely twilight. The park was emptying for the night and she was sitting in a particularly isolated spot. The old cannon was not near the children's play areas, nor was it near the lake or gazebo. It was, in fact, quite by itself on the south end of the large park, the main reason she'd chosen it for this meeting. But Keith wasn't there, and dusk was settling in quickly. There were lights in the park, of course, and heaven knew she wasn't normally a fraidy cat. Royal had a very low crime rate, but ever since the murder of that man who worked for Wescott Oil, Eric Chambers, everyone in town had been just a little bit on edge, a little more watchful. After all, the police appeared to be baffled and Eric's murderer could be anyone—even someone she knew!

That thought took her breath. Surely no one she knew could commit murder! Oh, what a horrible thing to think about at this particular time and place.

"Andrea?"

She nearly jumped out of her skin. Keith bounded around the bench and sat next to her. "Sorry I'm late. Just as I was about to leave, I received an important phone call. I couldn't cut it short. A business thing."

A "business" thing solely about Dorian Brady, which Keith couldn't possibly explain to Andrea. It was Sebastian who had called with the unnerving news that Dorian appeared to be preparing to leave town. "It's not certain, Keith, but it's a possibility. We have to step up our surveillance." They had set a meeting for first thing in the morning.

"And, of course, business *always* comes first," she intoned.

Frowning because she sounded much more knowledgeable than was possible, Keith peered at her. The only "business" of his she knew about was Owens Techware, and he replied in that vein. "At one time yes, but not anymore." He turned on the bench and settled his arm along the top of its back.

His arm touched Andrea's shoulders lightly. She was beautiful in the dusky light, her complexion glowing with good health and her dark hair a perfect frame for her perfect face. Oddly, they were dressed alike, in khaki slacks and white shirts. It would have been fun to kid about the two of them in matching outfits, but Andrea didn't laugh easily these days. Something deeply personal kept Andrea walking a very straight line, in fact, and Keith had only bits and pieces of clues about what it might be. All he could think of was that her marriage hadn't been as magical as she'd tried to make him believe.

But he had as many questions about himself as he did about Andrea. Last night's kiss between them had sizzled, and he'd run. That still puzzled him and even made him wonder if he would run again.

At any rate, he wasn't making a pass at the moment, he was merely getting more comfortably positioned to view Andrea as they talked. "Actually, my ex called my dedication to business ruthless. She said I had tunnel vision," he added.

"You're sorry about all that now, of course."

"Sorry? No, I'm not sorry. I accomplished what I set out to do, and Candace knew who and what I was when we married. I didn't change, she did. While we were dating she couldn't praise and encourage my ambition enough. In her eyes I was perfect, and I was besotted enough to believe she meant it. Well, she meant it until after the ceremony and I swear to God that we weren't married five minutes before she started trying to change me into someone else."

"I'm sure you're exaggerating. Five minutes?"

"I'm not exaggerating by much, Andy. Answer me this, did you change your husband?"

"Marriage changes everyone to a certain extent."

"But did you deliberately *try* to turn him into someone other than the man you married?"

Andrea paused to think, to remember, and if she were to be totally honest, she would have to say yes, because she had tried desperately to make Jerry listen to his doctors. One could say she'd nagged him all the way to the grave.

Oh, God, what a morbid subject! "Let's talk about something else," she said sharply.

"My question made you uncomfortable."

"Yes, it did!"

"Which leads me to believe you tried as hard to change Jerry as Candace did me."

"Look, that's all over with, for each of us. I don't care to discuss your marriage or mine. It's certainly not the reason I asked you to meet with me."

"Okay, what *is* the reason?"

With tension tightening her every cell, Andrea stared off across the darkening park. Only a few people were still there, and they were sitting or strolling near the lake.

Finally, reluctantly she spoke. It might not be the best beginning to a conversation with such a blurred topic, but it was the best she could come up with. "I don't know who I am anymore."

Keith cocked his eyebrow. "And you're blaming me?"

"Maybe. The only thing I know for sure is that this…the discontentment and confusion I've been feeling lately were *not* part of my personality before the Cattleman's Club's charity ball." She turned her head to look at him. "If you're not to blame, what is?"

He returned her gaze and they sat without moving and looked at each other for a long time. Finally he said softly, "I never forgot you, Andy."

She jerked her head around to break their locked gazes. "You have no right to tell me that. It…it's only upsetting and I don't believe it anyway. You forgot me the minute you walked out after our big fight in college. I made a fool of myself screaming and crying and you had no more sympathy for me than you would've had for a dog with a splinter in its paw.''

''That's not true.''

''It bloody *is* true! Forget it. I don't want to talk about that, either.''

''Well, at least we're gaining ground through the process of elimination,'' he drawled. ''I expect that eventually you'll get to the topic that really brought about this meeting. I say bless it, whatever it is, because it's getting harder and harder for me to come up with an excuse or a ploy to see you. Of course, I can always hang around Kiddie Kingdom.''

She stiffened. ''I wish you would stop doing that.''

''I know you do, and if you'd start seeing me…as in man takes woman to dinner…or something of that nature…then I wouldn't have to attend your classes. Those kids sure are cute, though.''

''When did you start liking children? Or even seeing them and admitting they are part and parcel of this world, for that matter?'' There was nothing complimentary in her questions or tone of voice.

''I didn't,'' he said flatly. ''Until now. What I'd like to know…and have asked myself more than once…is why I never wanted kids and now…'' He stopped, because he'd only recently been having these peculiar thoughts about sons and daughters, wondering why nearly everyone else he knew wanted babies and he never had. ''I really don't know my own mind on that subject,'' he said quietly.

''Except for the fact that you never liked kids and now you do. Maybe you're in the process of becoming a nice guy. Have you considered that possibility?''

He let out a surprised laugh. ''Andy, I've *always* been a nice guy.'' He crooked his arm behind her and gently touched her hair.

''No, you weren't, and please don't start getting all touchy-

feely.'' She slanted her head away from his hand. "I'm here to talk, nothing more.'' Was that true? she wondered. Just sitting next to him was warming her blood, so maybe all that need-to-talk stuff was pure nonsense.

"So talk,'' Keith said. "Tell me what's on your mind.''

Andrea swallowed nervously. How did a woman discuss really personal problems with the guy causing them? There really was only one way, wasn't there? By beating around the bush?

"I...I've been wondering if you, uh, remember my parents,'' she said, stumbling over her own tongue because she never had been a proficient liar.

"Your parents?'' Keith frowned, for she'd really surprised him with that remark. "Well, I guess I do. Not very clearly, though. And more from a child's point of view than from later years. Do you remember mine?''

"Yours?'' she said densely, before grasping his side of this strange conversation. "Oh, your parents. Well, yes, I have some memories of them.''

"Is that why we're here, meeting in a public place to discuss our parents? Andy, that's pretty weird,'' he said teasingly.

"I know it is,'' she replied grimly, not at all amused by his attempt to make her laugh. She immediately realized her mistake, for she could feel his eyes boring into her, looking for answers. She'd aroused his curiosity, and there wasn't a reason in the world for them to be talking about their parents. Especially since she'd requested this meeting and given him the impression that she needed to talk about something important.

She forced a laugh, because now she was boxed in and *had* to play along. "It's *very* weird,'' she agreed with false cheerfulness. "But my childhood memories of Mother and Dad are so sketchy that lately I've been bothered by it something awful. Unlike you, I remember their later years better. It's the kid stuff that eludes me. Would you mind telling me what you recall of them? Tell me anything...events...things they said…things you might have overheard or seen by accident.''

Keith was truly taken aback. After last night he'd expected some sort of discussion, possibly accusatory and disapproving about one of two things, his kissing her or his *not* kissing her more.

But he decided to play along and see where this led. ''Andy, my childhood memories are mostly about us, you and me. Both your parents and mine are shadowy background figures. Hell, my folks were so busy with social obligations that I rarely got to eat dinner with them. Dad was a dynamo, I recall that quite vividly, and Mother shopped.'' He laughed and sounded genuinely amused. ''She shopped in Houston and Dallas and New York and Paris. Can you even imagine making shopping the highlight of your life?''

''And my folks?'' she prompted.

''They were around more, but I think you answered mostly to the housekeeper, or whatever she was. Yes, I'm sure of it. She was a heavyset lady that came outside and called your name every hour or so. Do you remember her?''

''Mrs. Dorsett! We called her Ducky Dorsett behind her back because she waddled when she walked. I haven't thought of Ducky in years.'' Andrea was beginning to get a real sense of the distant past. ''My mother was a very beautiful woman,'' she murmured.

''Was she?''

''Extremely beautiful. I have boxes of photos and snapshots in the attic to prove it. There's one of her and Dad in my bedroom, and I swear they both look like movie stars. He was handsome and she was glamorous, with never a hair out of place and always, *always* dressed to the nines. Now I remember that very well.'' Andrea laughed quietly and added nostalgically, ''Sometimes when I went into a room where she was, she would say, 'There's that dirty little girl of mine,' for I was forever making mud pies or doing something outdoors that soiled my clothes.''

Keith chuckled softly. "We started out clean every morning, but we sure never worried about getting dirty."

"Very true."

Was this innocuous conversation actually the reason for this after-dark meeting? Keith wondered. He couldn't make himself believe it. This had to be about last night, about why he'd kissed her so passionately and then abruptly left. But how could he explain it to Andrea when he didn't understand it himself?

Gently he took her hand. "You're really thinking about last night, aren't you?" he said in a low voice.

She turned her head to look at him. "I've thought about it, yes. Haven't you?"

"Constantly."

She was glad he'd forced the issue. It was time to *stop* beating around the bush. "Keith, what happened?"

"I wish to hell I knew."

"But…" They had only scratched the tip of the iceberg, and she wanted to keep talking.

It had gotten so dark that Keith could just barely make out her face. All the same he could tell how troubled she was. He hadn't been kind last night, and she deserved better.

"I'm sorry," he whispered.

"That…that's it, all you can say about it?"

He searched for an addendum to his apology. "You said that you haven't been happy since the charity ball. I hope you know that it wasn't my intent *ever* to make you unhappy."

"Did I say unhappy? I believe I said confused and discontented."

"Well, a woman could hardly be in a rollicking happy mood if she's all confused and dissatisfied."

"Did I say dissatisfied? Stop putting words in my mouth, for heaven's sake. The ones I used are disturbing enough. I certainly don't need your suggestions to add to the list. Besides, why would you even think the word *dissatisfied* in connection with me?"

"Because of last night," he said in a low, barely audible voice. "I wish I hadn't left when I did. I've wished it all day. We wanted each other...we *needed* each other...and for some crazy, incomprehensible reason I walked out instead of doing what my heart and body ached for. I'm still aching, in case you're wondering."

"I...I'm not," she whispered, too deeply shaken to do anything but lie. Certainly she couldn't admit to the aches and yearnings she'd endured and tried so hard to ignore all day. All of last night, as well. Desires she'd never felt so intensely before were the reason she was on this park bench tonight, after all, the *only* reason she'd returned his phone call, in all honesty.

"After the explosive passion between us last night, I find it pretty hard to believe that you don't give a damn about my feelings tonight. Andy, I *care* about you, won't you at least consider that?"

"How can I worry about your feelings when my own are overwhelming me?"

"They are?" Keith moved closer to her and curled his arm around the back of her neck. "Sweetheart, if you only know what hearing that does to me."

No! She couldn't pretend everything was all right when it wasn't. She jerked loose of his embrace and got to her feet. "I'm in an emotional quandary and all you can think of is..."

Keith had gotten up when she did, and he put his arms around her and pulled her up against himself. "I can cure your emotional quandary," he said gruffly before uniting their lips in a breath-stealing kiss.

At first Andrea tried to push him away, but then she began kissing him back, exactly as she'd done last night in her kitchen. Moaning deep in her throat, she leaned into him. He slid his big hands down her back, cupped her buttocks and urged her forward. What she felt against her belly was perfectly normal and not surprising; what *she* felt because of such undeniable proof of his desire made her dizzy as a spinning top.

"Andy...sweet, sweet Andy," he whispered raggedly between hungry kisses.

Was *he* sweet? No, she couldn't call him sweet. He was big and sexy and overpowering her senses. She wanted what he did, and to worry over *why* seemed utterly silly. What did it matter when her body was reacting all on its own?

But when he unbuttoned her shirt and buried his face in the cleavage of her breasts, she gasped, "Not here, Keith. Not in the park."

He didn't argue. Instead he buttoned her shirt, took her hand and began leading her to the parking lot and his car. His SUV, actually, with its marvelous fold-down seats. It took him about one minute to create a lovers' nook in the back of his vehicle, and since his windows were tinted against the glare of the hot Texas sun, no passerby would be able to see in.

She didn't say no when he beckoned her inside, but she did steal a long, shaky breath. It was time she knew it all, felt everything she should have felt in college with him.

She wasn't thinking with her brain at all. Her body was directing the play, every act of it, and it did not want to say *no*. She lay down with him, and when he removed his shirt, rolled it into a ball and put it under her head for a pillow, she laid her hand on his cheek and whispered, "Maybe you are sweet."

"What I am is on fire," he said thickly, and spread himself across her legs and warm, sexy body to take her mouth in a kiss that conveyed the truth of his words. His bare skin was hot, and his heat even came through his pants. She reveled in that heat, for it intensified her own.

Gasping for air between kisses they wriggled out of their clothes. Andrea had never made love in the back of a car, and she suffered a momentary regret over doing something at her age that she probably should have done twenty years ago. Unquestionably she should have experienced this urgency of wildfire desire before, whether in a car, a bed or leaning against a wall. Oh, yes, she'd read about this kind of feeling, this wild lovemaking, she just hadn't experienced it herself.

She dug her fingertips into Keith's back and writhed beneath him, absorbing every tiny nuance of hot bare skin deliciously chafing hot bare skin.

Keith groaned silently. He didn't have protection with him. Why would he? It was pretty lax of him to be without it tonight, though, because he'd known in advance that he was meeting Andrea and had still been frustrated as hell over his stupidity last night. He should have been prepared for what was happening, given all that had been going on between them since the ball.

But he wasn't prepared, and he would cut off his tongue before telling Andrea they couldn't make love. Besides, would a baby upset the applecart for him? It sure would have in times past, but now?

Hadn't he recently read somewhere that many, many women were choosing to have their babies after forty? Why, Andrea wasn't *even* forty yet, so she would undoubtedly create an incredible child.

"I adore you...love you," he whispered against her lips.

She knew he'd said something, but she was in another world, one in which everything was sensation and pleasure and joyful surrender, and she didn't ask him to repeat it. She gave him everything she was, her heart, her soul, her body, without even knowing how deeply she was involving herself in the dangerous game of truly great sex.

When he entered her she cried out. He froze in alarm. "Andy...darlin'...am I hurting you?"

"No...no." Her head moved back and forth on her shirt-pillow, and she clutched at him. "Don't stop...don't stop," she moaned.

He tried to be especially gentle, but he couldn't be, not when it was Andy beneath him, the woman he'd wanted all of his life. Nearly blinded by passion and the fierce pounding of his own blood, he rode her hard. Her legs rose to encircle his hips, and as dazed as he was he was still aware of every sound she made, from her gasping little breaths to her hoarse cries of unabashed pleasure.

And then she cried out, "Oh, Keith...Keith..." and he knew she was almost there. He held himself in check through sheer willpower, and when she went over the top, so did he. They rocked together for an eternity, it seemed, squeezing every drop of pleasure from their simultaneous release.

But that particular eternity ended, as that sort of bliss always does, and Andrea found herself sweaty and wide-eyed, pinned beneath Keith in the back of his SUV in Royal Park.

Eight

After dropping Andrea off, the drive home didn't take long, nor was there much traffic. That was a relief, as Keith couldn't keep his mind on the road no matter what he did. This night's events were burned into his brain, all but blurring his vision, certainly making concentration on anything else particularly difficult. The physical effects he felt were surprising and confusing. After such incredible lovemaking he should be relaxed and serenely happy, and instead he felt tight as a drum.

After driving Andrea to her home from the park, he'd asked to go in with her. She had stammered out a few words, "No...please...not tonight," and he'd experienced the strangest rush of relief. That was something to wonder about: Why in heaven's name would he be relieved over Andrea's haste to end an absolute dream of an evening?

Keith's eyebrows nearly met in a troubled frown. There was something terribly wrong in his attitude at the moment, but what was it? Certainly he wasn't afraid of serious involvement, was he? For days he'd done everything but stand on his head to capture Andrea's notice, to regain her attention, to make her see him as she once had, and he'd succeeded, too, or they never would have made love. And now, when everything seemed to be going his way, he was fearful?

"Preposterous," he muttered. Hitting the remote control that opened the iron gate securing his driveway, he drove in, pushed another button and opened one of the four doors on his garage. He walked into his house with a scowl on his face, for he didn't like the direction of either his feelings or his thoughts.

His relationship with Andrea was different from any other. Vastly different from that he'd had with his ex and those he'd had with women he'd dated before and after his marriage. Actually, he hardly remembered them; they simply hadn't been important. He respected women but...but *he loved Andrea!*

That was the crux of his startling misery, he realized in one fell, rather shocking swoop: he was totally, madly and almost painfully in love with Andrea. He'd suspected it before, but there were miles of variances, discrepancies and disparities between suspecting something and knowing it for fact. Doubts and what-ifs had flown the coop, completely deserting him. He was on his own now, a man who had fervently pursued one very special woman, had reached the finish line and was now in a sweat over what to do next.

He didn't understand himself and it was a foreign, discomfiting sensation. What he needed was some time to sort through this whole thing, to figure out what was really going on in the pit of his stomach and to come up with some answers.

Instead of going to bed, Keith wrote a note for Gabriella, phoned Sebastian to tell him that he wouldn't be at tomorrow morning's meeting and where he'd be if he was truly needed, packed a bag with some changes of clothing, then carried it and his briefcase out to the garage. He drove from town heading south, refusing to look at his departure as running away. There was nothing wrong with a man taking a few days by himself to do a little soul-searching.

At least, that was what he kept telling himself.

Andrea awoke at two in the morning, uneasy and apprehensive. She lay still and listened, wondering if some outside noise had brought her out of a sound sleep so abruptly, but she heard nothing unusual. Still not satisfied, she got out of bed and walked through the dark house. Everything was normal; obviously her middle-of-the night-jitters were internally caused.

Well, she thought with a sigh, why wouldn't she have jumpy nerves? Actually, it was surprising that she'd gotten any sleep at all tonight.

Then, suddenly, she knew what had awakened her: a dream. It was vague and fuzzy now, mostly unconnected images of the past, not frightening, certainly not eerie enough to pull her from sleep, and yet it had. She didn't normally pay much attention to dreams, but considering her free and easy behavior with Keith in his SUV—and the emotional turmoil with which she'd fallen asleep, wasn't she bound to have suffered a few disturbing dreams?

Doubting that she would sleep again right away if she went back to bed, and with a decided sense of nostalgia, she went to the attic and returned to the living room with an armful of family photo albums. Before starting on them, though, she went to the kitchen, prepared a pot of herbal tea—she certainly didn't need caffeine tonight—and finally settled down on the sofa with tea at the ready and the stack of albums.

Some rated only a quick glance and she turned the pages swiftly. But then she came to the one filled with snapshots of her. Who had taken all of these she wondered—her mother, her father, Mrs. Dorsett?

Almost immediately she realized that Keith was in nearly every picture with her. A little brown boy, usually without a shirt, often without shoes, making faces at the camera or caught unaware while in the midst of a game. There he was in his pirate hat, Andrea thought with a soft smile of remembrance. For a while one summer they'd been on a pirate kick and their fort had been a ship at sea. For weeks they had fought off imaginary bad pirates—they'd been *good* pirates, of course—and saved innocent people from their evil clutches.

As she turned pages, the boy got bigger. She must have been growing, too, but her growth wasn't as obvious as Keith's. His shoulders became broader, bony for a while, then gradually filled out with muscle. He'd been a handsome little boy, a beautiful, adorable child, to be perfectly honest, and he'd grown into an extremely handsome adult. He had remarkable good looks, above-average intelligence and an athletic, muscular body. Andrea had to admit he was pretty much the perfect specimen.

She picked up her cup for a swallow of tea. Keith should have had children. He would have fathered incredible children…attractive, smart, active little replicas of himself. Of course, his ex-wife's genes would have shown in their children, as well. What was her name? Andrea couldn't remember the woman's name, but she did recall how pretty she'd been. And only from a few brief sightings, too. Funny what one stored in one's memory banks, Andrea thought.

For instance, the fact that she and Keith had made love without protection last night. Not that she would ever forget one second of last night. How could she, when she was so torn between resentment for having missed the blood-boiling excitement of wild, raw sex for so long and an uneasy joy over discovering her sensual side again?

Andrea sighed, for she hadn't encouraged one single man's interest since Jerry's demise. There'd been several very nice men who had asked her out, or at least given her the impression that they would like to ask her out, if she would only give them some indication of interest. She hadn't, of course, not ever. Her hands-off attitude had always served her just fine, but now she wondered about it.

She pondered that for a while, then for some reason again mulled over Keith's carelessness about protection. Not that he'd been the only careless person in that passion pit of a vehicle he owned. After all, she was as responsible for what they'd done as he was.

But surely she needn't worry about pregnancy, need she? Frowning suddenly, she got up and raced for a calendar.

"Oh my God," she whispered after calculating dates. She was smack dab in the middle of her fertile period. Feeling weak as a newborn kitten she stumbled back to the sofa and collapsed. She could be pregnant this very minute! What if she was? What if she and Keith had made a baby at Royal Park?

Andrea's body was suddenly taut with nervous tension. Just how would Keith take *that* bit of news, should it be true? Why in God's name hadn't he been concerned about the possible outcome of unprotected sex? Had he simply gotten too carried away to remember protection? That explanation made the most sense, although it really made no sense at all. Mature men and women did not take chances like that.

You did!

Yes, she had, and if she *had* conceived…? Her heart began pounding. A baby? A child?

Stacking the photo albums on the far end of the sofa, Andrea curled her legs under her to think about this very startling possibility.

At the same time something began coalescing in her brain…all the fragments of her thoughts since scanning the snapshots…Keith's beauty and intelligence…the odds of his fathering beautiful, healthy children…her excellent health. She could be pregnant with Keith's baby, and could any woman hope for a more physically and intellectually perfect father for her child?

But he didn't love her, and she didn't…well, she couldn't possibly love him, could she? Not that she hadn't loved him in the past. She'd all but worshipped the ground Keith Owens had walked on, but she'd buried all of those lovely feelings after the night of their big fight.

Why, it was utterly ridiculous to even wonder if she loved

Keith. What she felt was simply desire, just her response to his ability to transport her to the stars with kisses and surely the most incredible male body in all of Texas.

They had proved their feelings—or lack of—in the back of Keith's SUV, hadn't they? Sexual desire had run rampant, but love? Romance? No, indeed, there had been neither of those emotions spurring them on.

If she really were pregnant, should she even tell him about it? He might figure it out, but would he care? One thing was certain, she would not marry a man she didn't love and who didn't love her merely because of a child. She knew how to raise a child without a father. Dozens of women right here in Royal were single moms doing a very good job of it. And who understood toddlers better than a nursery-school teacher?

But what would she tell her friends? Pouring more tea into her cup, telling herself to calm down and not succeeding, she pondered people's reactions to her having a child without a husband.

But it was such a simple solution, really. Women all over the globe were having babies with the use of sperm banks. That was what she could tell her friends, prepare them ahead of time for the big event, in fact. "I want a child and I'm going to that fertility clinic in Dallas." Everyone would understand; everyone would *accept,* because her friends knew how much she adored children. A few might be surprised that she would go to such lengths to have a baby at her age, but perhaps her age would work in her favor. After all, how many years did she still have to conceive, carry and give birth to her own child?

And Keith probably wouldn't care even if he *did* figure it out. He'd wanted her sexually, perhaps he always had. It was entirely possible that one time in her arms was enough for him. She might never hear from him again!

Andrea's heart sank. Considering his sweet good-night kiss after driving her home and then his plea to come in with her, once probably wasn't enough. It was undoubtedly going to be up to her to end their relationship and put plenty of time between tonight—if she was actually pregnant, of course—and the future.

Could she do it? She had mastered her facade of dignity and decorum to protect and guard her privacy, but she could not claim to be overloaded with courage. This would take a shocking amount of deceit. Not just once or twice, either, but for the rest of her life. She couldn't factor leaving Royal in her plan, for it was home and the thought of living anywhere else, where she knew no one, was horrifying. No, she would stay put and should her and Keith's paths cross in the future—it was bound to happen—she would deal with it.

It all seemed so feasible, so possible if she kept her cool. Envisioning telling Keith that she was pregnant and watching him wriggle out of any sort of permanent arrangement because he was going to be a father would be more painful for Andrea than not telling him at all.

And so, she decided again and with a tear in her eye, if it were true she would have her baby by herself and raise it by herself. Tears suddenly dribbled down her cheeks. She'd given up long ago on ever having a child, but here was her dearest wish in the palm of her hand, or it seemed to be. Something very powerful—instinct, female intuition—told her that she *had* conceived tonight. She'd heard women say, "I knew I was pregnant the moment we made love," and now she knew exactly how they had felt. She wept with both joy and sadness.

She finally returned to bed and eventually slept again, but what had seemed sane, sensible and attainable in the middle of the night seemed nothing short of appallingly dishonest in the morning. Rubbing her eyes wearily, totally discarding her ridiculous notion of being pregnant after making love only one time and then deliberately keeping it from Keith because he didn't love her, she hauled herself out of bed, changed to running clothes and left the house. But she ran with more care, as she knew she would do everything until she found out if she was pregnant or not.

A long hot shower felt wonderful when she got back, and after some fruit and cereal for breakfast she got dressed for church.

That Sunday morning she drove past the church she usually attended and took the road to Midland. It was only fifty miles away, and she would make the eleven o'clock service. She did that occasionally, but never had she made that drive with such a heavy conscience. The serenity of the lovely old church and the beauty of the holy songs from the choir soothed Andrea's troubled spirit.

Back in Royal she decided to stop at the diner for lunch before going home. After locating a parking place only a short distance from the eatery, Andrea went in. If one wanted to touch base with stability or some sense of longevity, this was the place to come, she thought as she looked around for an empty booth. The Royal Diner never changed. Various employees had come and gone through the years, but the cracked red Formica that topped counter, tables and booths was almost comforting in its constancy. Also, any patron who had eaten there before knew that Manny, the cook, served up some mighty fine fare, especially his burgers and coconut cream pies.

Andrea walked to the only empty booth, sat down and then took note of the other people in the place. Recognizing several, she smiled, nodded and tried to look as cool and collected as she usually did. The courtesy was returned, but no one got up and came over to her booth. Glad that the other patrons were only acquaintances and she wouldn't have to get involved in any sort of conversation, she waited for the waitress.

A glass of water and a plastic-coated menu were set in front of her. Andrea looked up to say thanks and saw Laura Edwards, who seemed to be even more haggard than she'd been at the Cattleman's Ball.

"Hello, Laura," Andrea said quietly, forgetting her own problems for the moment.

"Hello."

"You remember me, don't you?"

"Yes, ma'am. Would you like a few minutes to look over the menu, or are you ready to order now?"

Andrea frowned slightly, for Laura's entire demeanor was distant and unfriendly. "I'll order now...a hamburger, well done, and a chocolate malt."

"Thanks." Laura hurried away.

Andrea felt truly rebuffed, but Laura's unnecessary coldness only made Andrea more certain than ever that something was terribly amiss in the waitress's life. Laura had lost weight, and the circles under her eyes evidenced a rocky road of some sort; those signs pointed to an abusive relationship in Andrea's opinion, for she'd seen that same haunted, scared-rabbit expression on the faces of battered women who'd sought safety at the New Hope shelter.

Sighing over her helplessness with Laura—neither she nor anyone else could ease another person's burdens if they refused all offers of assistance—Andrea turned her thoughts back to her own worries. If Keith decided to stay hot on her trail, there was no way she could keep him away. Hadn't she tried to do exactly that since the ball? She could decide to ignore him *and* tell him to leave her alone till she was blue in the face and he would still keep turning up like a bad penny, if he chose to. What did he want from her, other than the obvious?

Thinking of herself as any man's sex toy made her feel squeamish in the stomach and she hailed Laura. When the waitress came over, Andrea asked, "Is it too late to cancel my order? I'm not feeling very well."

"Came on you just like that?" Laura intoned.

"I'm sorry, but there's no way I could eat...anything. If you can't cancel, I'll just pay for it now and leave."

"Let me check with Manny." She hurried off.

Andrea took a sip of water and tried to will away the nausea. Everyone has problems, she told herself. You certainly can't get so upset that you become physically ill over yours.

Laura came back. "It's fine. You don't have to pay."

"Thank you, Laura." Andrea laid down two one-dollar bills. "For your trouble," she murmured.

"You weren't any trouble."

"Laura, do you still have the card I gave you the night of the ball?" Andrea had to ask. Whether Laura wanted help or not, she had to offer it.

"I...think so."

Andrea quickly dug in her purse. "I'm going to give you another one. I know something's wrong, and while I suspect what it is, I can't be sure unless you talk about it. At the same time I understand your reluctance to confide in anyone. But if things get too bad to deal with on your own, please, please call me."

Laura took the card and slipped it in a pocket of her uniform. "Thanks, Andrea."

"You're welcome." Andrea slid from the booth.

"I hope you feel better."

"I'm sure I will." Actually, Andrea started feeling better the second she was outside. It must have been the smell of all that greasy food, she thought as she began walking toward her car. She'd have a bowl of soup at home. Besides, she really wasn't all that hungry.

She had so much to think about that the afternoon flew by without her realizing it. It was about seven that evening that Keith's silence began to seem unusual. He really didn't give a damn about her, she thought morosely, not even a little, nor did he respect her enough to call the morning after. The entire *day* after, to be more accurate.

After an hour or so of beating herself up with that sort of self-inflicted misery, something finally gelled in her brain. Keith hadn't called because he wasn't going to call. Not ever again. He'd gotten what he'd wanted all along, and that had been the end of it for him.

Andrea had considered that scenario before, but now that she believed it with all her heart, her legs got shaky and she had to sit down. After a few minutes her pulse rate had quickened fearfully and her throat had gotten too dry to even swallow. Hurrying to the kitchen for a glass of water, she stood at the sink to drink it while tears coursed down her cheeks. *Keith had gotten the only thing he'd wanted from her!*

"You fool," she whispered raggedly, nearly choking on a sob. Why did this hurt so much? Wasn't it what she'd wanted all along?

Or had she really been hoping for the opposite and kidding herself?

Nine

Two weeks later, Andrea tended her class of toddlers with only half her mind on them; the other half was focused on that small empty chair at the back of the room and the painful fact of Keith's ongoing silence. She was past cursing herself for a fool and now she merely felt empty.

Using flash cards bearing numbers and letters of the alphabet in bright colors, she numbly went through the motions of testing her little ones' level of recognition. Later, when she read to them she recalled how enchantingly Keith had read the "cluck-cluck" story. Wondering if she should really believe that he'd suddenly started to like children, as he'd told her, Andrea pursed her lips angrily.

Oddly, anger revived her pride and sense of dignity, and when it came time to leave for the day she exited the building with her head held high and not so much as a glimmer of hope that Keith would be waiting for her in the parking lot. He wasn't, of course, and she got in her car and drove home actually relishing the fury she felt. She might never get the chance to tell him face-to-face how much she despised him, but then again she might, and *that* would give her boundless pleasure!

By the middle of the week, Andrea was weary of living on rage.

That morning, she had driven to an unfamiliar shopping center with a massive drug store and purchased two home pregnancy tests. The drive back to Royal had been conducted with a great deal of anxiety, all because of those upcoming tests. She wanted to know and she *didn't* want to know, and it bothered Andrea terribly to be so ambiguous. But this was not a trivial matter. This was quite possibly the most *un*trivial undertaking of her life.

The first thing she had done when she'd gotten home was to check her voice mail. There had been brief messages from two women friends who had merely called to chat. That was all. Andrea had been disappointed that Keith had not called, even though she wasn't sure she wanted to hear from him.

She sat on her bed and gingerly took out the two packaged pregnancy tests, almost as though they had teeth and the ability to bite her. This was nerve-wracking, she acknowledged, probably because she wanted so passionately to have a child. She'd *always* wanted a child, and if the tests came out negative she was going to be terribly disappointed.

An hour later she was weeping quietly, but not from disappointment. Both tests had come out positive: she was pregnant! She had some decisions to make, primarily whether she was going to follow her usual routine of not teaching during the summer months. Kiddie Kingdom was open year-around, with two- to four-week break intervals scattered among four approximately two-month terms. Most of the school's employees took one of those terms off and Andrea had always chosen the summer term for her annual break. This year, of course, was different from any other. Her decision now wasn't about taking one break but whether she should completely retire from teaching. First, though, before she did anything so rash as that, she planned to see an obstetrician. She was convinced of her condition, but she *was* thirty-eight and this was her first child. Making sure that everything was all right seemed crucial to her.

Her friend Rebecca surprised her with a phone call and some questions that afternoon. "Andrea, is something wrong? I haven't heard from you recently and I was worried. What's the matter, Andrea? Surely you know you can tell me anything."

The only thing Andrea knew for sure was that she couldn't tell anyone anything. Her friends were good people, wonderful people, but Andrea did not feel close enough to any one of them to let go of her natural reticence and tell all. After all, there'd been nothing to confide for years and years. Her life had been an open book until Keith had manipulated his way back into it, and what could she say about that? "Oh, by the way, I made love with Keith Owens in the back of his SUV, and now I'm pregnant." The mere thought of such a confession gave her cold chills.

Andrea's fury finally diminished enough to permit her to wonder about Keith. While she pondered her teaching career and a summer break versus retirement, something in the back of her mind urged her to locate him. Just knowing where he was and what he was doing would relieve a lot of her tension. And if by some small miracle she actually got to speak to him, she could coldly and calmly tell him what a louse he was and then hang up. Why it would be so satisfying to lambaste him with dignity and then be the one to hang up, she didn't know, especially when she considered the situation. But she was just so darned hurt by his ongoing silence. How dared he treat her so shabbily?

She finally did it. Nervous and rattled, she dialed Keith's home number. His phone rang twice before a female voice said, "Owens residence."

Andrea asked for Mr. Owens and heard, "Mr. Owens is not at home. Would you like to leave a message?"

"Uh, no. No, thank you. I'll call again, uh, later." Andrea

hung up and weakly fell into a chair to recoup her courage, for now that she'd made one call, she *had* to make a second.

It took about five minutes to gather enough courage to dial Keith's computer software business. A woman answered again. "Owens Techware. How may I direct your call?"

"I need to speak to Mr. Owens, please."

"I'm sorry, but Mr. Owens is not in."

"Oh. Well, do you know when he will be in?"

"I'm sorry, I do not. Would you care to leave your name and number?"

"No, thank you." Again Andrea hung up. He wasn't home and he wasn't at his place of business. Could he possibly be hanging out at the Cattleman's Club today?

She looked up the number and dialed it. "Cattleman's Club," a male voice said in her ear.

"Hello. I'm trying to locate Keith Owens. It's not an emergency but it is important that I speak to him. Is he there, by any chance?"

"Nope. Sorry. Do you wanna leave a message in case he comes in? We got a bulletin board, you know. I could post your call."

"No…no, thank you." Shuddering at the thought of her name and phone number being posted for all to see on a bulletin board in the Cattleman's Club, Andrea hung up for the third and final time. Either Keith was out of town or in hiding.

She opted for "in hiding," the big jerk.

Even with the consistent use of sunscreen, Keith's skin had darkened to its usual summer mahogany. He'd driven non-stop from Royal to the house he owned just south of the border in Mexico, a long drive but worth it. His flat-roof, southwestern-style house was situated within a stone's throw from the lapping waves of the Gulf of Mexico and had been his private getaway since his divorce. A small fishing village was within walking distance, and he took the walk every day to purchase fresh fish, shrimp, locally grown vegetables and homemade bread baked by some of the ladies of the town. He also bought Mexican beer and ice, and he spent most of his time on the verandah of his house sipping ice-cold beer and watching seagulls and the water.

After two weeks he still had no answers. Or at least not the definitive answer he wanted, the one that satisfied the restlessness of his mind and body. Thus, the question remained to haunt him: Why had he so fervently chased Andrea and then gotten confused when he caught her? Good Lord, he'd even had thoughts of babies and Andrea as his wife before everything went weird on him.

Yes, everything, he told himself. Andrea hadn't been at all thrilled over his successful breach of her personal ethics, which she'd conveyed very effectively by refusing his request to go in with her after he'd driven her home. That night with Andrea, she'd been hotter than live coals in the back of his SUV and then, for no reason he could give logic to, she'd reverted back to pure ice. Strange woman, no doubt about it.

At any rate, the only conclusion Keith had reached in two weeks of soul-searching was that he and Andrea probably weren't destined to be together. Wasted time, he thought, wasted effort. He might as well go home.

But the next morning was so incredibly beautiful, with a cool breeze off the Gulf and that perfect view from his verandah of the water and small fishing craft that he never tired of looking at, he decided to stay for one more day.

It was that afternoon that he thought of asking Andrea to join him. Maybe they still had a chance of making things work for them. She might very well refuse for legitimate reasons, or she could simply cut him cold, but he really did want to figure the two of them out and why shouldn't she be here going through the stress of the inquisition with him? Besides, she might enjoy the view as much as he did.

After debating the issue until long after the sun had set, he finally placed the call.

Andrea was reading—or trying to read—in bed that night while gentle, soft music wafted from the concealed speakers of her CD system. She'd seen an obstetrician that day, been given the ultimate medical test for suspected pregnancy and a thorough physical exam, been told she was definitely pregnant and in excellent health and part of her was quietly thrilled.

But that other part, the one that mightily resented Keith Owens, wouldn't relent and let her retain one word she read. Soothing music generally relaxed her, but it wasn't working tonight and neither was the book. The text kept getting lost among the uncountable questions about Keith that felt like rodents gnawing great gaping holes in her brain. Questions about herself, as well. She could hardly classify herself as unaccountable for letting Keith seduce her, after all.

Who was she now? Certainly not the same well-adjusted, clean-living Texas widow she'd been before the Cattleman's Club charity ball. *That* woman would never have succumbed to a man's desire in the back of his vehicle!

Sighing, Andrea closed her book; there was little point in staring at it. She was reaching to turn off the lamp on the nightstand when the phone rang. It was a bit startling, for her friends rarely called after eight at night and it was now after ten. Still, it did happen occasionally, and so she unsuspectingly picked up the receiver and said a calm, quiet, "Hello?"

"Hi, Andy. How are you?"

It was Keith. Her pulse went crazy and she suddenly couldn't breathe. "Hold on a second," she gasped. "I...I have something on the stove." She held the receiver against her chest, cursed her stupid lie and wondered frantically how to deal with this. He hadn't called for...well, it was over two weeks...and now he expected...what?

Wait a minute, she thought. Did it matter what he expected from this call? She had herself to think of, her trampled-in-the-mud pride to resurrect, her child to protect from the unmitigated selfishness of its own father. Yes, this was an opportunity to call Keith foul names at full volume and let him know how much she loathed him, but would that *really* make her feel better? Probably not. One thing might, though.

Raising the phone to her ear, she spoke with studied calm. "Sorry, my pot of gravy runneth over."

"You're cooking gravy at this time of night?"

"A lovely brown sauce, really. It's for a late supper with a…friend. Oh, excuse me for another second, Keith." This time she laid the receiver on the bed, got up and walked around the room, murmuring as she went. "Do have more wine. Supper's almost ready and feel free to turn up the music, if you wish." She had a volume control in her bedroom and she gave it a twist so Keith would be sure to hear the music.

Then she returned to the bed and retrieved the phone. "I'm sorry. What were you saying?"

"I wasn't saying anything." Keith was trying to keep his wits intact, but what he was hearing over the telephone was damned confounding. Andrea was obviously entertaining a man with wine, a late supper and some extremely sensual music. She had never invited *him* to a late supper, damn it, and dining alone together late at night conveyed a special intimacy. "I was *trying*, but I wasn't getting very far," he added, sounding very much like a sullen child.

His tone of voice truly gladdened Andrea's heart. Gladdened her entire system, for that matter, her wounded female pride, especially. "I can only apologize again," she said without the slightest inflection in her voice. He would get nothing from her tone, not so much as a hint of her true state of mind. This was much better, much more gratifying. "You must have had a reason for calling," she said.

"What about your lovely brown sauce?" he asked sarcastically.

"It's fine. Everything's fine. Now, why did you call?"

"Because I had the misguided notion that you might enjoy a few days in Mexico."

Andrea's eyes widened in surprise, but she had to play out the hand she'd dealt herself. "When are you going?"

"When am I going? I'm here!" he shouted. Andrea had to put her hand over her mouth to stifle the laughter bubbling up in her throat. "I've *been* here for two weeks! Didn't you notice I wasn't around?"

"Well...no, actually. You've really been out of town for two weeks? Time goes so quickly, doesn't it?"

"Are you putting me on?"

"Now Keith, why would I do that?"

"I have no idea. Anyhow, would you like to come down here for the weekend? I have a nice house on the Gulf, and it's peaceful and quiet and a great place to unwind."

"It sounds marvelous, but I've made all sorts of plans for the weekend and I couldn't possibly disappoint my friends, especially on such short notice."

"But you don't care if you disappoint me."

"Why on earth would that disappoint you? You've obviously been enjoying yourself for all this time without my company. I'm sure the weekend will be equally enjoyable. Keith, I really must sign off. It was very nice of you to call."

"Wait! Don't hang up yet! Andrea, *please* come down. You could fly to Corpus Christi and I would pick you up there. Andy...we could..." He stopped to clear his throat. "...talk. I think we need to talk. I do, anyway. I've been doing a lot of thinking, but the problem with looking for answers by yourself is that everything's one-sided."

Recalling her own long hours and days of probing for answers, she could only agree. "That's true," she said, still speaking without inflection, although there was a noticeable ache in the vicinity of her heart and she honestly felt like crying. "But when one lives alone...for myself I wouldn't have it any other way...but I know that living alone makes for some very solitary conversations. I'm sorry, Keith, I simply cannot get away this weekend. I have to say good-night now. Pleasant dreams." She hung up.

But instead of feeling great over finally besting Keith at his own double-dealing game, she buried her face in her pillow and bawled like a baby.

In Mexico, watching the reflections of moonlight on the Gulf waters, Keith scowled and pondered the phone call. He hadn't known Andrea was seeing other men, although he was aware that her circle of friends included men. She had never seemed unhappy, he mused with a sinking sensation. They hadn't run into each other that often through the years, but when it had happened he'd never seen signs of unhappiness on her beautiful face. She didn't sound unhappy tonight, either, not when she was cooking and entertaining a male guest at this hour.

Then the full impact of what he'd discovered with that phone call hit Keith. Andrea was serving one special guy a candlelit supper, and that was so painful it was physically jarring. Jealousy ripped through his guts like a hot knife through butter. Unable just to sit there and take it, Keith jumped up from his chair on the verandah and headed for the beach.

His mind ran faster than his legs, torturing him with another spate of questions without logical answers. Whatever was going on in Royal, did he have the power to do anything about it? For that matter, regardless of that painful burst of jealousy that still hadn't completely disappeared, did he really *want* to do anything about it?

Maybe he should have stayed in Royal and figured everything out there. Fat lot of good running away had done. He'd been in Mexico for weeks, and did he know his own feelings any better tonight than he had during that long drive from Royal?

Realizing that he was now looking at his departure from Royal as *running away*—the night he left he wouldn't even consider that possibility—caused him to grimace.

"You are one sorry piece of humanity," he muttered.

Andrea could not remember a time when her emotions had been so jumbled. She'd had her bouts with love before, and with sorrow and grief, of course; losing loved ones—her parents and Jerry—had put her through an emotional wringer three different times. But she was discovering a new type of misery that seemed to spring from within her very own self. Thinking of the baby helped, but even that joy didn't cure her malady.

Finally she unearthed and faced what was really at the core of her melancholy. She'd been applauding herself for putting Keith in his place when he called, and she deserved no applause. She'd been unkind and deceitful with that stupid charade and she regretted her playacting.

Why was there so much pushing and pulling between them? Right now they should *both* be thrilled and happy about their baby. Instead she couldn't even tell him about it. Nothing would ever convince her that he hadn't gotten all unnerved over their passionate interlude and run away to nurse his wounds…or his *imagined* wounds. He'd begun his campaign the night of the ball and hadn't let up for a minute. And he'd won the trophy, too, hadn't he?

No, she thought then. Keith hadn't won the trophy, she had!

When she looked at the wide-screen perspective of this whole affair, she was astonished that Keith ran off to Mexico instead of swaggering all over Royal crowing about how his irresistible machismo had finally overcome Andrea O'Rourke's defenses against men in general and him in particular.

And now he believed there was another man in her life. How could he believe anything else after her dramatic rendering of "The Widow and the Late-Night-Supper Lothario?" It disgusted Andrea that she'd resorted to such cruel tactics. If she'd been so bent on giving Keith some attitude and even on letting him know what a low-down dirty dog she considered him to be, she hadn't had to make a run for the best-actress-in-Texas award like some melodramatic teenager. She was a mature adult, after all. *And* a mother-to-be!

If Keith *hadn't* relentlessly pursued her she would not be a mother-to-be. She supposed he deserved thanks, not censure. Besides, maybe a woman needed a man like Keith to lean on during bad times and to rejoice with during the good times.

But that of course would involve telling Keith everything, and she really didn't know how he would take the news of impending fatherhood resulting from one belated sexual conquest. Somehow, given what she remembered about him, she really couldn't see him jumping up and down for joy.

By Friday afternoon Andrea had gotten herself into such a state that when a woman friend, Linda Vartan, called with a casual invitation to drop by her house on Saturday for grilled steaks and ribs, to be cooked by her husband at poolside, Andrea couldn't say yes fast enough. Sitting around and wallowing in all sorts of emotionally dark dungeons for two days was an unbearable prospect. Thus, on Saturday she tried on her two new bathing suits—purchased during a shopping trip to Dallas in April—and took her time in deciding which one to wear to the Vartans' today.

It was gratifying to be firm and fit enough for a two-piece suit—all that running really paid off—but she'd also bought a stunning one-piece in jewel-tone colors and she decided on it. After taking it off and slipping into a comfortable cotton wrapper to do her makeup, she sat at her dressing table. She had just applied a glossy light-coral lipstick when the front doorbell rang.

"Oh, for pity's sake," she mumbled. She wasn't dressed for company, nor was she expecting any. She had to leave for Linda's in less than an hour and she didn't want to get hung up with some inconsiderate caller and arrive late.

Rising from the dressing-table stool, she tied the sash of the wrapper and took a look at her reflection in the mirror. She was not appropriately clad for this time of day, but she was decently covered. Sliding her bare feet into terry slippers, she hurried to the front door. Whoever was out there was an impatient soul, because he or she was practically leaning on the bell. Terribly annoyed over that alone, Andrea jerked open the door. Then she stood with her mouth open and stared at Keith, who sported the most incredible tan and looked positively devastating in white duck pants, sneakers and a white-and-blue polo shirt.

Keith stared, too. Andrea was wearing a rose, teal and royal blue something or other. It looked to him like some kind of robe, or maybe a bathing suit cover-up. Hell, he didn't know what it was, other than damned sexy, which sort of ticked him off. She hadn't known *he* was coming by, so she was obviously dressed for that late-supper jerk.

"Aren't you going to invite me in?" he asked gruffly.

"I...I'm getting ready to...go out." Andrea felt hot all over and wished she could free her overheated body from the wrapper and get some air on her feverish skin. He was much too handsome with that tan. Damn it, he was much too handsome *without* a tan! And all she could think of was how he'd made her feel in the back of his SUV.

"I'm sure you can spare a few minutes."

"Uh, no, I really can't. Not if I'm going to be on time."

Her flushed face said more to Keith than the words formed by her full luscious lips. She was *afraid* of inviting him in! She knew what could happen...and just might...if they were alone in her house. And that robe or casual dress or whatever it was she was wearing looked pretty darned flimsy. In fact, it looked to him as though she had nothing on under it.

He cleared his throat in an attempt to ignore—and reverse, if possible—what was happening in his pants. "You should either let me come in or shut the door in my face. It's hotter than hell out here and your air conditioners are running full throttle."

"Oh, yes, you're right," she mumbled. One didn't stand with the door open in hot weather in Texas or, she supposed, any other place where temperatures soared above the century mark. She stepped back and opened the door wider. "Come in...but as impolite as it sounds I have to say that you can't stay for long."

He stepped inside and she closed the door behind him. "I hope you understand. I believe I mentioned having plans for the weekend when you called the other night."

"I understand more than you think."

She stiffened from sudden fear. He didn't know about the baby, did he? How could he know? Deciding that he couldn't and it was ridiculous even to think he might, she asked coolly, "What's that supposed to mean?"

"Nothing and it wasn't true, anyhow. Andy, I don't understand a damn thing that's been happening between us. Okay, you have plans and I won't ask you to break a date. But how about later on today? Or this evening? I just want to talk. In fact, I'm being eaten alive by a need to sort things out. I can tell you right now that's never happened to me before, and I have got to get to the bottom of it."

She didn't completely believe him, but it didn't matter. If she agreed to another talk, it would probably evolve into the same thing that had occurred between them at the park. She really had to keep her distance from him. "I'm sorry, but I'm sure I won't be home until quite late this evening."

"That's okay. I could come back then." He had things to do anyhow, such as talking to the guys and catching up on their recent observations of Dorian. Also, he needed to work on breaking that code of Eric's.

"No!"

"Why not?" He moved in and put his hands on her waist before she could get out of his way. "You don't have a stitch on under this thing, do you?"

"That's none of your business," she whispered and realized that she was trembling, just from his touch, his scent, his nearness.

The color of his already dark eyes seemed to get darker. "I want you, but you know that, don't you?"

She swallowed nervously. He *did* want her again. She *hadn't* been a one-night stand. Oh, how could a once clear-thinking woman be so confused that she couldn't tell up from down, or right from wrong?

He pulled her forward and kissed her hard on the mouth. Then he let go of her. "I promise I won't do that tonight. I meant it when I said we needed to talk. That's all we'll do, I swear it. See you tonight.''

He walked out of her house and left her standing in her own foyer with a benumbed expression on her face, as though she had no clear concept of what had just taken place.

Ten

Andrea was relieved to see so many cars when she arrived at the Vartans', as she had worried about being the only guest when she wasn't in a party mood. The presence of others— quite a few, by the look of it—took a major burden off of her.

She tried to appear relaxed and delighted with pool volleyball and tasty grilled food. Her heart just wasn't in it, though, and she mostly sat in the shade of the patio roof and thought about the sameness of every function this crowd created and attended. There simply was no excitement in that lovely backyard and it made Andrea sad to realize it, for she had enjoyed these genteel people and their conventional attitudes and well-bred activities for quite some time. Finding fault with them now was terribly unnerving.

In truth, the word *excitement* had taken on a whole new meaning for Andrea. It occurred to her with a touch of sadness that she was no longer satisfied with her solitary lifestyle. Most of her friends were married or had seriously committed partners. The few single men in the group were well-read and great conversationalists, but they were…well, dull.

Andrea flushed. How could she sit there and deem her unwed male friends dull? From behind her dark sunglasses she studied one fellow—Jim Bailey—whom she'd known for years. He had on perfectly hideous bathing trunks that were so long and baggy they reached his bony knees, and he had a caved-in skinny chest with about three hairs more than the few on his balding head. Jim was a super-nice guy, always ready for a long discussion on any subject anyone mentioned, and Andrea liked him, but was he even slightly exciting?

No one was, she thought dismally. No one but Keith.

Was he back in town for another romp in his SUV? Maybe he'd class it up a bit by luring her into an actual bed, but the result would be just as degrading if all she was to him was the pushover of the week. Would he treat her differently if he knew she was carrying his child? She honestly didn't know the answer to that question, which depressed her further.

Wishing the day away one minute and hoping it would drag on forever the next, Andrea put in hours of phony good cheer and forced smiles with her friends. Around five, the Vartans took cocktail orders from their guests, and Andrea's request for plain ice water drew some good-natured teasing, which she laughed off.

Drinking was not normal routine for this crowd's social affairs, but a pool party was always a bit looser than those events held in more formal settings and it wasn't long until some of them were dancing to Latin music and having a high old time.

Andrea was coaxed into dancing a few numbers, but then she returned to her chair in the shade and her ice water. But it had felt good to let go and forget—if briefly—Keith and his brand of excitement and all of the worries and heartaches that had unbalanced her equilibrium since the ball. While the others got sillier and funnier, Andrea mostly watched from her chair on the patio. Even without her complete participation she knew that this party had turned out well for the Vartans.

It was around seven when she began feeling queasy. She should have gone home hours ago, and would have if Keith hadn't been lurking in the shadows again. With so much on her mind, Keith asking questions—or making another pass— was more than she'd wanted to deal with. Thus, she had stayed outdoors longer than she should have. The heat was stifling, even in the shade, and her occasional dips into the pool to cool off hadn't done much good.

Making the rounds she said goodbye to everyone and then shocked herself and her friends by getting so dizzy she reeled and nearly fell flat on her face. No one laughed. They rushed to help her to a chair, to ask how she felt, to talk about heat sickness, to comment that she must not have felt all that great all day because, after all, she'd refused even a glass of chilled wine. Andrea hemmed and hawed and finally said something about the heat being a little much for her today, then announced that she was fine now and really should go home.

But everyone agreed that she shouldn't be driving. Not when she was already dizzy, for heaven's sake. She really couldn't argue that point, not when she felt like hell and longed almost desperately for the cool comfort of her bedroom.

And so she left her car at the Vartans' and let Harry Vartan drive her home. Andrea tried to focus on him as he chatted, but her head was spinning too much to concentrate on anything. Harry walked her to the door of her house, unlocked it for her and then asked, "Are you going to be okay if I leave now?"

"Yes. I just need to lie down." Her head had started throbbing painfully, also caused by the heat, she was sure, and she blessed the obstetrician she'd seen for giving her some samples of safe medication in case of a headache.

"Are you sure?" Harry asked. "I could come in and check the house for intruders, if you'd like."

"Thanks, Harry, but my security system is very good." Even lightheaded and unfocused she managed to press the right sequence of numbers to disarm the security system.

"Well, if you're sure. Linda and I will drive your car over tomorrow."

"Thank you. Good night." She shut the door and then stumbled her way through the house to her bedroom. Doffing her swimsuit, she fell on the bed without a stitch. Her ceiling fan was running and the moving air felt cool and wonderful on her hot skin. Even without medication she began feeling better. And sleepy, she realized drowsily. Very, very sleepy.

She was almost asleep when the front doorbell chimed. "Go away," she mumbled, for she was in that lovely zone of half sleep, utterly relaxed and almost floating.

A few minutes later she heard someone rapping on the French doors that led from her bedroom to the patio. She opened her eyes to see Keith looking in at her. It was getting dark and she couldn't clearly make out his expression, but he seemed to be totally mesmerized by the sight of her.

Keith *was* mesmerized. Never in a million years could he have imagined Andrea lying on her bed stark naked. He'd come around her house because she hadn't answered the doorbell. Suspecting that she'd decided not to see him tonight and swearing not to let her get away with it, he'd knocked on every door he'd come to.

This was the big-prize door, he realized. He'd hit the jackpot with this one, because there she was, naked, incredibly beautiful and…and… He frowned, because she was just lying there, not in a panic because he *was* outside filling his eyes, or even acting as though she was aware that he was outside. What was wrong with her? Something was. The Andrea he knew wouldn't just lie there and let a man—*any* man—watch her when she was naked as the day she was born.

"Hey," he called, alarmed now, and he rapped on the French door again.

"*Go away!*" Andrea yelled. She honestly didn't care if he

saw her naked; she cared that he was out there trying to get in!

Keith's jaw dropped. "What's wrong with you?" he called. "Are you sick or something?" Pounding on the door he called her name. "Open up, Andy, or I'll call the police."

He'd call the police? What on earth for? She tried to make sense of his threat, but she couldn't do it. Suddenly furious, she slid off the bed, walked to the door and unlocked it.

"What the hell are you doing?" she demanded to know when the door was open.

Keith stepped inside. "What the hell are *you* doing?" he retorted. Was she drunk, he wondered. But no, she didn't look, act or sound tipsy. "Apparently you had a good time today."

"So what if I did? What're you doing here?"

"We had a date."

"We most certainly did not!" Her nudity suddenly became an embarrassment, and she turned to go and put something on.

But Keith had other ideas. "Not yet," he said softly and stopped her retreat by pulling her into his arms and lowering his lips to hers. The warmth of her struck him hard, and the kiss that had begun soft and gentle became hungry. Holding her naked was an incredible high, and he wanted nothing more than to *continue* holding her.

But why in heaven's name was she naked in the first place? Too curious to ignore the questions stacking up in his mind, he broke the kiss, raised his head and peered at her in the dimming light.

"Something happened today," he said. "You're different."

Andrea wished at that moment that she could tell him about the baby. She was dizzy again, she realized, but not from the sun this time, although Keith's heat was almost as potent.

"No, I'm not," she said, denying her difference only because she couldn't be honest. But she was different, all right, in more ways than one. Standing naked in his arms was so foreign to the woman she'd once been that even she found it hard to believe.

Keith slowly slid his hands up and down the smooth warm skin of her back. "Why were you lying in the dark like this?" he asked softly.

Andrea sighed. If she told him one truth she might tell him everything. Besides, they had *not* had a date tonight. She had not agreed to his coming over and talking tonight. He was being his usual pushy self, and she was letting it happen again!

"Keith, don't!" She escaped his embrace and went for a robe.

Keith walked over to the bathing suit she'd dropped on the floor and picked it up. "It was a bathing-suit party?" he drawled, conveying sarcasm with tone of voice and his most pronounced Texas accent.

It annoyed Andrea. "Don't grill me," she snapped. "Whatever I did today is none of your affair." She realized that her head was beginning to ache again. What she needed more than anything else right now was a shower. But first she had to get rid of Keith. "Would you please leave? I want a shower, a bite to eat and then a good night's sleep."

"Take your shower. Who's stopping you?"

"Damn it, Keith, don't you know when you're not wanted?"

He laughed. "Go take your shower. I'll wait in the living room…or maybe the kitchen."

She gave up. It was either that or stand there and argue with him, and the only time she'd gotten the better of him—and that really hadn't been an argument—was the night he'd called from Mexico. Maybe her deceit that night was part of the reason she shut up and marched into her bathroom. Without a doubt she was truly sorry about it.

Twenty minutes later when she exited the bathroom she was so much more alive it seemed a small miracle. Her headache was gone, she had no sign at all of nausea, and, in fact, she even felt a little hungry. The aroma of coffee reminded her that Keith was somewhere in the house, but she felt stronger and more able to deal with him. Figuring there was little point to maidenly modesty after that major-motion-picture nude scene before her shower, she donned a light-weight, knee-length robe, ran her fingers through her still-damp hair and left her bedroom. The odor of coffee became stronger as she walked to the kitchen. It was probably where he was lying in wait of her, she thought dryly.

She was right on the money. Andrea hesitated at the doorway for a moment and saw a very cozy little scene—Keith seated at the kitchen table with a cup of coffee and the newspaper, which still resided where she'd left it that morning. He either heard or sensed her presence because he looked up and smiled.

"Hi."

She walked in and headed for the coffeepot. Her "Hi" wasn't nearly as friendly as his had been, but at least she hadn't immediately shrieked at him. She pulled a cup from a cabinet and picked up the coffeepot.

Keith got up and hurried over to her. "Let me do that. Go over to the table and sit down."

"I am perfectly capable of filling a cup with coffee!" She proved it.

"Fine. Just trying to help. Are you feeling better now?"

"I'm feeling just fine, and I'm going to have a piece of toast."

"Sit down with your coffee and I'll make your toast."

"I don't have a broken leg, for God's sake! I'll make my own toast. *You* sit down."

"Okay, okay, you don't have to get mad. I was just trying to help." Keith returned to the table and sat down.

"Would you like some toast?" she asked stiffly.

"Sure, I'll have a piece. Thanks."

His thanks annoyed her, as well. Obviously she was easily annoyed tonight, but why wouldn't she be? Why didn't Keith just leave? Surely he had to realize how distressing all of this was for her.

When the toast popped up, she put each slice on its own plate and brought them to the table dry. After getting her coffee she returned to the table and sat down.

"I'm eating mine dry. If you want butter or jelly, they're in the refrigerator. Just help yourself."

He grinned, got up, went to the refrigerator and then into a drawer, and ultimately returned to the table carrying a jar of strawberry jam and a spoon. Seated again he spooned jam onto his toast.

Andrea couldn't help glaring at him. "You seem quite amused over something. Care to share it?"

"Well, when I first saw you on the bed without a stitch on, I thought you might be tanked."

Her voice dripped icicles. "I do not get 'tanked,' and for your information, although it's none of your business, all I drank today was lemonade and ice water."

"Maybe you should've tried something stronger. That ice water can be lethal."

"Funny, very funny. You probably thought I was looped because you're so familiar with the malady."

"Well, not really. I haven't overdone it in that department for quite a spell, actually."

"How marvelous," she drawled. "Mr. Perfect."

"Now, that hurts. Even if you had been tanked I wouldn't have judged you for it, Ms. Andy Pandy. And why wouldn't I think you might have drunk a little too much when you'd been at a bathing-suit party all day?"

His blatant enjoyment of this discussion was more than Andrea could take and remain calm. "You didn't *know* it was a pool party, so don't pull that high-and-mighty face and act as though I drink at every excuse! I *rarely* drink, and then it's only a glass or two of wine."

"Hey, don't you think I know that? The whole town knows it."

"Yes, and now the whole town also probably knows you're here, in my house right now!"

Keith laughed again. "Not the biggest crime of the century by anyone's measure," he remarked. He liked her cosmetic-free face. With her hair finger-combed and no makeup she looked like a young girl. "Andrea, I'm not going to apologize for sticking around in case you needed someone. Before you showered, you looked pretty shaky."

She sipped coffee from her cup and dared to meet his eyes. "I'm not shaky now."

"I can see you're not."

"Well, doesn't my excellent physical condition give you any ideas?" She was hoping he would take another extremely unsubtle hint and go home.

"One or two," Keith said softly, then just sat and looked at her. Finally, when he could see that she was getting uncomfortable over such a long silence and his unbroken gaze, he changed gears and said, "I was remembering something when you were showering. Do you remember when I filched a bottle of crème de menthe from my father's liquor cabinet and we drank it in the fort? I think we were about thirteen. You didn't like it very much and only drank a little but I chugged most of the bottle...playing big man, I suppose. Anyhow, I got sick as a dog and you took care of me. We both knew if I went in the house that sick my folks would cart me off to the emergency room, and then everyone would know that not only had we drunk alcohol but that one of us had stolen it.

"So you took care of me. You brought in pans of water and clean towels...you must have sneaked into your house for them...and you kept bathing my face, and I kept heaving. It went on all afternoon and we were scared spitless of what would happen when we had to go in for dinner. But by then I was weak but able to walk into the house without giving anything away. I remember telling my folks some story about getting too much sun and losing my appetite over it. I recall receiving their sympathy instead of their wrath, which made me feel guilty, but not guilty enough to confess the truth.

"The point of all this is that you helped me through a killer hangover one time and tonight I wanted to help you, even though you're so dead certain you didn't need it. It was no big deal, Andy, so don't turn it into one."

"What we did as children cannot be compared to our behavior as adults."

"Why not? We're taller and maybe a little smarter, but we're basically the same people. When one gets down to hard facts, the only real difference between a man and his childhood is the type of games he plays. I doubt that women are all that different."

"You certainly have your own way of interpreting things. Speaking for myself, which *you* cannot do, there are few similarities in the person I am now to the child I was so many years ago."

"There are more similarities than I can count. You really can't see them? Or feel them?"

"I'm not overly pleased with every memory, as you seem to be. For one thing I was your shadow as a kid. I'm certainly not that now, nor would I ever be again."

"Andy, you weren't my shadow, you were my pal, my best friend, my buddy."

"Until high school," she said with an infusion of ice in her voice, for his transformation from best buddy to swaggering, conceited star jock in high school still smarted. "You turned into a complete jerk in high school."

"Well, hormones do strange things to boys. Girls, too, I suspect. Anyhow, everything evened out in college, didn't it?"

"To a point," she grudgingly agreed.

"That point was the bedroom door, wasn't it? Damn, I wanted you. I ached for you, every damned minute of every damned day. And you kept talking about your wedding night. I sure as hell hope Jerry O'Rourke appreciated your virginity, because you guarded it like something sacred. And maybe it was. Maybe you were right and I was wrong about that. It's hard to know now. So much has happened since then. You got married, I got married..." Keith's voice trailed off.

Then he spoke again. "But we're not married to other people now, Andy," he said softly. "And neither are we kids. Our connection is still strong, just as it was when we *were* kids, only it's even better now because we both have more sense. I do, anyway."

Her hands were under the table, in her lap, and she couldn't stop herself from wringing them. It was the perfect opportunity to tell him that he was going to be a father, if she was ever going to do it. That was the problem. Was she going to stand firm on her decision to keep him in the dark?

"Andy," he said quietly, "don't you love me even a little bit?"

She'd been wondering just how personal he was going to get with this conversation but never could she have dreamed up a question like that.

"I...Keith...don't ask me things...like that," she stammered.

His gaze never lost its directness. "Why not?"

Andrea was sure her face was crimson, because it felt hot as a furnace. It angered her—she couldn't let something like this, probably just another ploy to get her into bed, influence her decision about the baby—and she spoke harshly. "All right! I suppose some childish part of me will always...I can't bring myself to use the word *love,* so I'll say that because of our intertwined pasts, some part of me will probably always care for some part of you."

"And that's the best you can give me?" Keith sat back, shoved his hands into his pants pockets and stared across the table at her with a challenging, unblinking gaze. "I've been thinking of a lot more than that, you know."

"No, I'm afraid I don't know. What's more, I don't *want* to know." Shaken, she got up for the coffeepot, which she brought back to the table, and refilled his cup. She'd intended to fill hers, as well, but more coffee suddenly didn't sound so good.

Returning the pot to the coffeemaker, she was taken completely by surprise when she felt him standing right behind her. In the very next instant his arms moved around her and his face was in her hair.

"No, Keith," she whispered shakily, but his hands were moving over her breasts, her waist and abdomen. He pressed his body against hers and continued to caress her through her robe. She told herself that she didn't want this, but her heartbeat had gone wild and an intense craving in the pit of her stomach was torturing her. She felt the way she had that night in the park, all soft and boneless, and she could not stop herself from leaning against him.

"Andy...sweetheart," he whispered raggedly. "If just touching each other makes us want so much, it has to mean something."

"You...you're not just touching me," she gasped as his hand worked up the front of her robe. "Keith...we can't keep doing things like this." How could she maintain a charade about the child in her womb and keep on making love with its completely-in-the-dark father? She groaned.

"We can, damn it, we can!" Keith exclaimed.

"You're just as...as leery of commitment as...I am." She was on fire from the gentle but extremely knowledgeable stroking of his fingers between her legs.

"Maybe...I'm not sure anymore. Why do you think I left town? After we made love that night I needed to do some heavy-duty thinking."

"And?" she whispered thickly while moving her feet farther apart to give him all the space he needed to keep on working his magic. She'd never been so overcome—not even in his SUV—from one rather simple caress from a man. "Did you figure out anything?" Had he? Oh, if he only said the right things right now she would crumple and tell him everything.

"No. A man can't figure out those kinds of answers all by

himself. I should have stayed in town and talked to you. Opened up with you and begged you to do the same with me.''

She moaned with intense pleasure and totally forgot the theme of their conversation.

''Feels good, huh? Andy, we're almost like one person, don't you realize that? We were the same way as kids, always together, playing together, getting into trouble together. You must remember at least as much of it as I do.''

''Don't...don't talk now,'' she mumbled. She couldn't stand there a moment longer, not even with him doing all the supporting. ''Let's take this...out of the kitchen.''

''Are you inviting me into your bed?'' he whispered huskily.

''Don't put it into words,'' she groaned, afraid even to think, let alone talk. ''I'm telling you that talking right now will stop...everything.''

He didn't say another word. Instead, he released his hold on her, took her hand and hurried them both from the kitchen to her bedroom.

Kissing almost frantically, they began undressing each other. Tearing each other's clothes off was a more accurate description of their haste and hunger. Finally down to bare skin they fell on the bed together, wrapped in each other's arms. Andrea was so ready that she pleaded, ''Do it now. Please, do it now.''

Keith became so excited by her passionate request that he plunged into her at once. ''Andy...Andy,'' he repeated gruffly as he almost roughly moved in and out of her.

She was in another world, the same one she'd touched on in his SUV, but tonight it was even more mind-boggling. She writhed freely beneath him, giving him everything, following his lead and rhythm, and she wanted it never to stop. This had to be...love.

No! she thought wildly and immediately buried the word beneath layers of sexual pleasure. Love was something else.

This was physical sensation and love was…well, it wasn't this.

Keith too wanted it to go on forever, for once it was over they would have to talk again. Talking was the best medicine in most cases, but Andrea was so guarded with her inner thoughts that he was afraid of another dead end, or even of inadvertently angering her. She didn't take demands well, so he knew he had to be tactful in any discussion without appearing to be a wimp. He *wasn't* a wimp and never had been, but Andrea scared him. Not in a physical way, that would be too ridiculous to consider, but she was strong-minded and set in her ways, and he knew she could turn on him in the blink of an eye.

Except right where she was, under him and moaning and whimpering from the pleasure he was giving her. In bed, making love, he was the stronger. At least for the time being. Who knew the next time they made love? Andrea might take the initiative. He didn't doubt that she'd do anything she wanted to do.

There's the key! He became even more excited because unearthing what Andrea really wanted was the key to any future they might have together. Riding her harder, faster, he brought them both to the brink. She cried out his name…"Keith…oh, Keith"…and he knew the moment had come. In seconds they went over the edge, in perfect harmony again, which completely amazed him.

Supporting himself on his forearms so he could look at her face he said softly, "Do you realize what a rare couple we really are?"

Eleven

―――――

"A...couple?" Andrea echoed hoarsely. Out of all the words he'd just said, *couple* registered with the most impact. She didn't know to react to it. Could he actually be thinking of them as a couple? A *committed* couple?

She peered into his velvety dark eyes and realized that she hadn't seen them looking this soft and shiny since...well, she couldn't remember when. "Your eyes look like chocolate kisses," she had teased as a child. And he'd teased back by calling her "blue-color-crayon eyes." He'd even taken out the cobalt-blue crayon and shown her which one matched her eyes. She had giggled.

She didn't feel like giggling now. She felt like a puddle of something soft and oozy. He'd done that to her. He was the only man who'd done that so well, and maybe she should tell him that.

"You're looking awfully serious," he said with a bit of a grin. "Does the idea of our being a couple scare you?"

Andrea recognized it as his *teasing* grin. She'd seen it

often enough, after all, and it contained exactly the same amount of daring and fun that it had years ago. He wasn't committed to anything but his own pleasure, same as he'd always been.

She wasn't angry, just very, very hurt. She showed him nothing of her true feelings and smiled. "We're a couple, all right," she quipped. "A couple of nuts. Let me get up, please." For humorous emphasis she slapped him on his arm.

With a broader grin he rolled onto the bed. "Don't take your time," he told her as she picked up her robe and hurried into the bathroom.

"Funny," she dryly said over her shoulder. "You're a funny guy."

"And you're my sweetheart," he called out just as she was disappearing behind the closed bathroom door. Locking his hands behind his head, he lay uncovered and let the ceiling fan cool his feverish body. He was positive that he had never felt more contented or satisfied than he did at that moment.

Andrea took a quick shower and thought about his parting shot. She was the mother of his child, but she wasn't his sweetheart. At least she didn't feel that particular role.

But if she was so certain about that, why had she let him make love to her again? The first time had taken her by surprise, but today? No, today she'd been fully cognizant of the meaning behind his first touch. And now he was in her bed, waiting for her, probably with all sorts of erotic ideas whirling around in his head.

Trembling from so many emotions warring within her system, Andrea felt tears fill her eyes. This relationship had moved into emotionally dangerous territory. She had tried everything she knew to avoid this very thing, but Keith had kept coming, hot and strong. Then he ran away, then he came back, and then…? Well, who knew what Keith's next move would be? How could she risk her baby's future with such an on-again, off-again man for a father?

By the time she was ready to leave the bathroom she had

decided her most sensible course was to treat Keith and everything going on between them as ordinary adult entertainment—and *not* tell him anything. If at all possible, she would keep it light and shoot for laughs. *Yeah, you're just a laugh a minute these days.* The wry observation of the little voice in her head was somewhat discouraging, but it wasn't as if she had a week to figure this out. Keith was here now, she had to put on a happy face and act as though going to bed with him was no big deal.

Bracing herself, she walked into the bedroom with a smile. It was phony as a three-dollar bill, but only she knew that.

"Hey, you're dressed," Keith exclaimed.

"Hey, you're not! And I don't think wearing a robe constitutes being dressed," she retorted. "What're you going to do, lie there naked all night in hope of more action? Forget that, sport. I'm totally done in. See you in the kitchen...or wherever." She walked out with her own erratic but powerful heartbeat nearly choking her.

He was too much for a woman like her to deal with, she thought breathlessly. Lying naked on her bed like that, with every part of him in plain sight. No shame at all, no *modesty* at all.

In the kitchen she stuffed the half of her toast she hadn't eaten before into her mouth. Her stomach was as shaky as her legs, and she hoped the small piece of toast would ease that particular ailment. The table was really a mess, she realized, with dirty dishes and newspaper strewn all over it.

But she couldn't deal with that, either, and she left the kitchen and went to the den. Going to a window she looked outside at Keith's SUV in her driveway, but her bad nerves wouldn't permit her to dwell on that big masculine vehicle or the destruction of her reputation it had caused.

Finally she sat down and waited for Keith to show his face. She wasn't at all comfortable because she couldn't get past the seriousness of her situation and when Keith did appear she was going to have to act as though going to bed with him was no more than a bit of Saturday-night fun.

Fun.

Groaning quietly, Andrea put her head back. Her mind was swimming with thoughts, all of them disturbing. She was sitting in the same chair and wearing an agonized expression when Keith walked in.

"Oh, here you are," he said.

Startled, she drew a quick breath and composed herself. "I see you got dressed."

"An easily reversed process, leave us not forget." There was a devilish twinkle in his eyes, a true reflection of the joyful excitement he was feeling over the evening's events.

His gist was so apparent that there was no way Andrea could misinterpret it. *Remember to keep it light!* her little voice reminded.

"I suppose we could always make a contest out of who could get undressed the quickest," she drawled.

"I would win."

"You still believe you're the best, the fastest, the smartest, the absolute cat's meow, don't you?"

Keith chuckled. "The cat's meow? I haven't heard that in a long time."

He sat on the end of the sofa closest to her chair and Andrea's gaze moved from him to the opposite end of the sofa with its stack of photo albums. Her housekeeping, her almost obsessive penchant for having everything in the house clean, tidy and in its place, had obviously gone to hell the same as her moral standards had or else she would have put those albums away once she'd looked through them.

For some reason those albums being on the sofa instead of in the attic made her completely forget her vow to keep things light between her and this overbearing man. This distracting, conceited *male* who had grown up thinking he was the center of the universe. Why wouldn't he intrude on her life? On anyone's life, for that matter. When the entire universe revolved around you, you intruded on anything you wished without once thinking you could possibly *be* an intrusion. Oh, the gall of him, the bloody, damned gall!

She simply could not hold her tongue, and there was a caustic edge to her voice when she spoke. "I'm going to tell you something, Keith, which, given your massive ego, you won't want to believe, but when we were kids I *let* you win our swimming and running races. I let you beat me at checkers, chess and games. I deliberately fumbled the ball when throwing it so that you would throw it a greater distance than me. And I constantly fed your ego with praise for how much better at everything you were."

He looked first surprised then amused. "Now why would you manufacture a story like that? Anytime I beat you, it was fair and square."

"I knew you wouldn't believe me."

"Andy, I didn't *always* beat you."

"Only because I figured you'd catch on or even lose interest in our games if you won every time. I didn't want you losing interest, because you were my best friend and my hero. There was no one to take your place, should you go off and leave me behind." She paused briefly, then added, "Which is exactly what you did in high school."

"Well, teenagers can be cruel."

"Not *all* teenagers. You were a jerk, and if you had one honest cell in your body you'd admit it."

Keith grinned. "Since you put it that way, what can I do but admit it? I was a jerk in high school. There, does that make you happy?"

"Don't be absurd."

"Andy, I'm trying to be agreeable. What would you like me to say?"

"Well, for one thing you could say that you *knew* I was letting you win most of the time."

Keith couldn't help laughing. "But I didn't know, and I still don't. You played your heart out, whether it was a game of checkers or tag. Besides we were really young when we played together. In middle school I was on the softball team and you weren't. As I remember it, you joined the girl's volleyball team."

"And the soccer team, and the tennis team, and... Oh, what difference does it make now? Yes, in middle school we weren't constant companions. We couldn't be...except during summer breaks."

"So in truth," Keith said, "we began growing apart in middle school, not high school. Andy, you're right about one thing. What in hell difference does it make now?"

"Then you believe me? About my letting you win most of the time?"

"No, I don't believe you. I was always twice your size. I could always outrun and outswim you. I still could."

"You most certainly could not! Do you run almost every day, as I do? I could beat you with one hand tied behind my back."

"Or one foot?"

"Don't make fun of me!"

"Then change the subject. I couldn't care less which of us is the fastest runner."

"Well, you cared when we were kids!"

"We were *both* competitive, Andy." Keith wasn't grinning now. In fact he was getting more upset by the moment. In his opinion this was a stupid, adolescent conversation, and he wished he could get Andrea on another track. Still, he couldn't lie and tell her he believed that she'd let him win when they were kids. His good nature could be stretched only so far, even if it was the woman he loved doing the needling.

He sucked in a startled breath, not because his being in love with Andrea was a brand-new thought but because it seemed so permanently embedded now, so much a part of who and what he was, of who and what he wanted to be in the future.

A clap of thunder so loud that it seemed to rock the house took them both by surprise. In mere seconds the sky opened up and began spilling rain, sheets of rain.

Keith jumped up. "I think I left a window open."

He ran from the den and Andrea heard an outside door open and close. It occurred to her to get up and arm the security system so he couldn't get back in, but she merely contemplated the idea for a few enjoyable moments. Then, sighing, she got up and walked through the house to look out various windows at the severity of the sudden storm. It was while frowning at the sight of flowers bent to the ground from the heavy rainfall that she realized the headway she and Keith were making, regardless of the childish bent of their conversation. The childishness was her fault, she'd searched for a safe subject to discuss to keep his mind out of the bedroom, and she'd come up with that ludicrous tale of letting him win all the time. Small wonder he'd gotten miffed.

But if they kept talking…they'd covered childhood, middle school and some of high school…wouldn't they eventually get to the topic of their college relationship, at which time she could let him know how cruel he'd been? Wasn't that what she'd been wanting to say to him all along, certainly since the ball but also during all of those years after their breakup? This was her chance; she should take it.

Returning to the chair in the den she'd used before, Andrea wearily laid the back of her hand on her forehead. She wasn't physically tired, but the thought of fighting, arguing or debating the past with Keith again was emotionally exhausting. Should she really put herself through that to finally say to his face, "You were a wretched, cruel person that night." Would he care if she did say it?

Ask yourself this, Andrea O'Rourke, do you really want to run Keith off? Do you truly want to succeed in causing a division so permanent and irreversible that the two of you would go out of your way to avoid each other for the rest of your lives, just as you did the last eighteen years?

Andrea sighed. She didn't know what she wanted, except for one utterly impossible thing: to turn back the clock to the day she'd been told about the Cattleman's Club donation. If she could go back to that day she would tell the other New Hope volunteers that she could not attend the ball as the charity's representative and someone else would have to do it.

Everything that had happened concerning Keith since the night of the ball would be erased with that one small change of history. He wouldn't be here tonight; he would never have been here. Nor would they have met in the park, or ever made love. Her life would be serene again, the placid stillness of her daily existence would never have been disrupted.

But you wouldn't be pregnant. She wanted this baby. She wanted it more than she'd ever wanted anything.

"Andrea!"

"What?"

"I'm dripping water all over your laundry room. Bring me something to wrap up in and I'll toss my clothes in the dryer."

She got to her feet and called, "I'll get some towels."

"Thanks," Keith called back. He'd started undressing the minute he came in, so by the time Andrea appeared with an armful of clean towels, he was stark naked.

"Well, honestly," she drawled with deliberate sarcasm "You drop your drawers faster than anyone *I* ever knew." She set the stack of towels on the folding counter.

Keith grinned. "You just don't know the right people, sweetheart." Helping himself to what looked like the largest towel in the stack, he wrapped it around his hips and tucked it together at his waist. "There, all covered up again. How do you get this dryer going?"

"Probably the same way you get *your* dryer going."

"That's not something I do, Handy Andy."

"So we'll let Handy Andy do it, right?"

Keith shrugged. "I know it's a tough job, but someone's gotta do it."

"Who wipes your nose and washes your back when Handy Andy's not around?" Andrea turned the dryer dials and pushed the Start button.

"Believe it or not, I can manage to wipe my own nose. But back-washing's a whole other ball game." He moved closer to her—she was still facing the dryer—and put his arms around her. "I'll bet you're a hell of a back-washer," he said, burrowing his face into her hair. "Damn, you smell good. You *always* smell good. What kind of perfume do you use?"

"I rarely use perfume. All you're smelling is body lotion and…and shampoo. Keith, please, don't do this."

"Can't help it, sweetheart," he said huskily. "You're all I think about anymore."

"Which, of course, is the reason you fled to Mexico after our…uh, first time together."

Keith cooled down in the space of two seconds. He could lure her into bed again, of that he was positive, but there was still something huge and forbidding between them. It felt like a locked door, and even when they made love that door remained securely bolted. If their relationship was going to make it to the finish line—which seemed to be what he wanted, at least, it was what he wanted tonight—then he had to unearth the key to that lock.

Even as kids it hadn't been easy to get Andrea to talk about something she would rather not discuss. She'd been mule-headed stubborn as a child and it appeared to Keith that she hadn't changed much. Which made him wonder why she was willing to have sex with him when she'd made it so plain on numerous occasions that she'd wished he would disappear from the face of the earth.

He dipped his head and kissed the side of her neck and said softly, "Let's light the fireplace in the den and listen to the rain together." He let go of her.

"Uh, fine. Good idea." Andrea hurried from the laundry room.

Keith stayed right behind her, watched the delightfully feminine way she walked and wished that she were wrapped in a towel, too. Not that her robe was much of an obstacle, should they both get in the mood again. Maybe they would. What better way could a man pass a stormy night than to spend it with a woman who made him feel young and glad to be alive? Andrea did that for him. Yes, on second thought he was *certain* about their relationship reaching the finish line. All he had to do now was convince her.

"Since you're so helpless around a house, I'll light the fireplace," Andrea said as they walked into the den.

Keith smiled. "Yes, dear."

"How do you survive on your own?" Shooting him a rather disgusted look she turned on the gas and pushed the striker button. The flames leapt to life at once.

"Oh, I have plenty of help."

"You must."

"Paid help, Andy."

"Yes, well, one can buy anything with enough money."

"That's not true."

"Name one thing." She sat in the same chair again and Keith returned to the sofa.

"Love. Sex can be bought, even companionship can be bought, but not love, Andy."

"I'm sure you could buy a pretty good facsimile, considering how many single women would give their eyeteeth to nail a man like you."

"I'm special because of my bank account?"

"Uh, well, you're not unattractive, you have to know." *Especially with that dark tan and those incredible eyes. Damn it, do you* have *to be so good-looking?*

"So you think I'm attractive?" Keith asked innocently.

"Not nearly as devoutly as *you* think it, but yes, I see you as an attractive man."

"Devoutly?" Keith laughed. "You do have a way with words...or should I say subtle insults?"

"If you consider what I said an insult, how do you deal with the real thing?"

"Honey, one thing you are is the real thing."

Andrea bristled. "And what's *that* supposed to mean?"

"Only that you're the genuine article. Andy, it was a compliment."

"Well, since you don't know me well enough to judge me as genuine *or* phony, I really had no clue as to what it was."

"You really think I don't know you?"

"That's right. You don't know me any more than I know you. Everything between us is strictly superficial."

"Superficial? You're calling each of us depthless and our feelings trivial." He leaned forward. "Is what you feel in bed with me trivial?"

She cast her eyes downward, for his seemed too full of feverish emotions to comfortably look at. "What…would you call those kinds of feelings?"

"Not trivial!"

"Okay, fine. Answer me this. Why did you run off to Mexico after we made love in the park?"

"You actually said it without hemming and hawing."

"You're trying to turn the tables on me, and I'm not going to let you do that. Give me an answer."

Keith finally sat back, and he turned his face from her to the fireplace. "I wish I hadn't gone."

"Now you're going to play on my sympathy? No way, Keith. Why did you go?"

"I needed to think."

"About?"

He looked at her again. "About us. About you, about me, about what was happening between us. For all the answers I came up with I might as well have stayed here."

Andrea felt suddenly weak. "You…you must have found some sort of answer. You came back and…and…"

"And we made love again," he said softly. "Maybe we should get married."

She gaped, she gasped and she nearly stopped breathing. Rising, she went to the window and looked out, mostly at the rain running down the glass.

"I know you don't mean that, so why did you say it?" she said.

"Maybe I do mean it."

"But you're not sure."

"Oh, Andy, are you? Are you sure you want me out of

your life, or would you rather I hung around and we got it on every so often?''

She whirled around. ''Don't you dare talk to me like that.''

''Why in hell not? That's what we've been doing, isn't it?''

''Twice does not an affair make!'' Turning around again she found herself looking at her empty driveway. ''What did you do with your car?''

''I put it in your garage.''

''Next to mine?''

''Your car's not in the garage. Someone obviously drove you home today. It was probably your new boyfriend, the guy you cook fancy little suppers for at midnight.''

''You're jealous!''

''Am not.''

''You sound exactly like a sullen child, so don't try to con me, Keith. I don't care anyway. I do not have a boyfriend, and what you heard over the phone the night you called was precisely what I wanted you to hear. I lied, Keith. I wanted to get back at you. When you called I was in bed…alone…with the CD player on. I fabricated everything else.''

Keith slowly got to his feet. ''I never would have guessed it.'' He tried to smile but it came off as feeble. ''You didn't let me win that night, did you?''

''We're not in a contest, Keith.''

''What would you call it?''

''I've been trying to figure that out, and so, apparently, have you.'' She glanced back at the window again. ''Harry Vartan drove me home because I wasn't feeling well. He and his wife are good friends of mine and the party was at their house.''

''You weren't feeling well?'' Keith frowned. ''How come?''

Probably because I'm pregnant! ''Too much sun, I think.''

''Are you sure that's all it was? How are you feeling now?''

"Obviously I recovered or I never would have let you in!" she replied waspishly. This whole thing was really getting her down. Tell him...don't tell him. Ask him to leave...let him stay as long as he wants.

They looked at each other for a very long moment, and then Andrea's eyes filled. Wiping away leaking tears, she returned to her chair and sat down.

Keith sighed, shook his head then headed for the laundry room. His clothes were probably dry by now.

Twelve

Fully dressed again, Keith stood at a window in the den and watched the storm, visible through the many yard lights on Andrea's property. What he couldn't get past was Andrea's surprising deceit the night he'd called from Mexico. She'd been mad as hell or she wouldn't have gone to such lengths to make him think she was entertaining a man. Had his leaving town caused so much anger? Or was it—and this supposition was much more serious than his first—the aftermath of their making love in the back of his SUV?

Keith's frown intensified. He seemed to be suddenly bombarded by guilt and it was coming at him from all directions. He had pushed Andrea too hard. He'd kept after her and kept after her, completely ignoring her protests, and he could claim success, if luring a woman into bed was the yardstick with which he measured victory in a personal relationship.

But he hadn't only wanted sex from Andrea. In fact, he was annoyed by the mess he'd made of something that had started with the very best of intentions. Uneasy and troubled,

Keith wondered if there was any chance of setting them on the right track. He loved her. But for some reason he hadn't been honest with her.

"Damn," he muttered, shoving his hands into the pockets of his pants.

Glancing back at Andrea, Keith saw the distress on her face. His heart sank. Neither of them was happy with the way things stood between them, and if they didn't come to some sort of understanding, nothing was apt to change. Maybe tonight was do-or-die, he thought grimly. Maybe this was it—the real beginning or the bitter end.

He noticed the stack of photo albums on the sofa—they had piqued his interest when he'd first come into the den. Seating himself next to them, he transferred the top album to his lap and asked, "Is it okay if I look at this?" It was really just something to do until he thought of an opening line to get them communicating with no-holds-barred. Nothing else would alter the status quo, he now believed, nothing but complete and sincere honesty from each of them.

"Sure, go ahead," she said listlessly. She honestly had no fight left in her. Massive amounts of emotion, but not enough strength to put on a defense against anything Keith might do or say.

"Thanks." He began turning pages and his speed slowed to a snail's pace when he realized the snapshots he was looking at were all of Andrea, from when she was about five to— he took a quick peek at the album's last page—her early teens. And he was in almost every one of them!

Looking at those old photos brought back so many memories—most of which he'd long forgotten.

His interest surprised Andrea, and she watched him. Seeing Keith while he was so immersed, she could see both the boy he'd been and the man he was now, and for the very first time she began to grasp that they were one and the same. It seemed like a revelation of sorts, although of course he was the same person. Why wouldn't he be? It was just that she hadn't been thinking of him in that way. If she'd loved him so much before, she should love him still.

Did she?

Her heart began pounding, and she tried desperately to think of something else, something trivial, something that wouldn't rip her from stem to stern. He'd always been the best-looking male in her life, always! Andrea's breath caught. She'd loved and adored Keith the boy and, she had discovered, she loved and adored Keith the man, now.

Keith chuckled, startling Andrea out of her reverie. "What so funny?" she asked, relieved to have a distraction. Rising from her chair, she went to the sofa to see for herself which picture had made him laugh.

"Look at this," Keith said.

Andrea sat next to him to peer at the photo he was indicating. It was a snapshot of her draped in pink chiffon—she recalled that playtime outfit as some old curtains, although where on earth she'd gotten them was a mystery—and Keith in his pirate hat and brandishing a cardboard sword. They were about six or seven years old, she figured.

"Do you remember the day this was taken?" he asked.

"Well…no. Should I? Do you?"

"Yes, I remember it. We both got hell for playing doctor."

"We were playing doctor with you in your pirate hat and me in pink curtains? I don't remember that."

"We weren't in them for long." Again Keith chuckled. "After Ducky took this picture…"

Andrea broke in. "I was wondering who had taken all these snaps. Was it Mrs. Dorsett?"

"Mostly, yes. Anyhow, after she snapped us in our favorite getups that day, she went in the house and we returned to our fort. I'm not sure exactly how we evolved from pirate and harem girl to doctor and nurse…or maybe it was doctor and patient…but we got totally naked and were busily examining each other when Ducky appeared to announce that lunch was ready. The poor woman nearly had a stroke when she saw us."

"That's not true. You made that up. I never played doctor with you."

"Andy, why would I make up something like that? Hell, we were little more than babies. I honestly don't recall how we even figured out that our bodies were different, but it apparently happened and innocent little beings that we were, we were curious about the differences."

Andrea was unwilling to admit to something *she* couldn't recall at all. "I don't believe it," she said stiffly.

Keith laughed. "Fine, *don't* believe it. It's not important anyhow."

But it was. It was one more shared event—even funny when she really thought about it—and further proof that their life on the same cosmic plane had begun over thirty years ago.

He turned his head to peer at her; she was close enough for him to see the flecks of black in her blue, blue eyes. He also saw a mist of tears and an alarming intensity.

"Let's not blow this out of proportion," he said quietly, hoping to soothe her. Why a simple little memory from their childhood would bother her to this degree escaped him, but her agitation was obvious. After moving the album back to the stack, he put his arm around her and gently urged her head down to his shoulder. "It can't be that bad," he said softly.

"It…it's not bad," she whispered, "just disturbing."

She began crying, and her flood of tears soaked Keith's shirt in seconds. He was dismayed by so much emotion over a perfectly normal childhood incident, but he sat there, held her and let her have her cry while he gently stroked her hair. He hoped that this might be that beginning he'd deemed necessary for their relationship to progress, but he wasn't impatient about it.

Then, without warning, Andrea got up, mumbled "I'll be back," and left the room. Keith got to his feet and frowned at the vacant doorway. What had that trip down memory lane done to Andy? The only thing it had done to him was to give him a few laughs, but she hadn't laughed over it, she had cried.

Andrea walked in with a box of tissues. Her eyes were red from weeping and the tip of her nose was pink, but she was much calmer, and she sat in a chair and asked him to please sit down again. "I have something to tell you," she said.

Wary and more than a little concerned, Keith slowly sank to the sofa again. Something told him he'd been right. This was either a new beginning or an irreversible ending for them. He hesitated to speak at all, but she seemed to want to hear from him.

"Is something wrong?" he asked slowly, cautiously.

She thought a moment, then said, "Maybe something's right, but right now I don't know."

He frowned at her. "You're worrying me, Andy."

"I know." She dove in, head-first. "Keith...I...I'm pregnant."

Keith froze solid. His mouth would hardly form words. "You're what?" he finally got out.

"I'm pregnant," she repeated. She could see his throat bob up and down as he swallowed. While she'd expected some show of surprise, she had not anticipated an almost fatal case of panic. Was he wondering if he should get out of there and run like hell? That was what he looked like. She had finally faced the truth of her own feelings for him and decided that she couldn't possibly withhold the existence of his child from him, and he was reacting as she had expected. She was never going to learn, was she?

"You can...uh, know that this soon?" he mumbled.

The damage was done. As much as she wished it, she couldn't take it back. She squared her shoulders, looked him right in the eyes and said coldly, "I've taken several tests, seen an obstetrician and there's no doubt."

Life was beginning to return to Keith's benumbed system. She was pregnant. They were going to have a baby! My God, this was a miracle. Shocking, yes, but definitely a miracle.

He got up and walked over to her. "When did you know?"

She sank deeper into her chair because she didn't want him getting too close. "I knew it was a possibility after our night in the park. I knew for certain once I took the tests."

He was so tall, and he was looming over her. She knew he was beginning to guess it all, and rather than let him flounder for a while longer, she decided to give it to him straight.

"I wasn't going to tell you at all." The fire in her eyes dared him to say something insolent or insulting.

His dark tan became noticeably lighter by several shades, right before those blazing eyes of hers. "You're not serious?"

She was *not* going to back down on this, or cower and act all weepy and wrong. From the look of him, as though she'd just taken away his very last toy and now he would *have* to grow up, she never should have even hinted at her condition.

"I'm *very* serious," she snapped. "Why should I want to tell you? You ran away like a scared little boy after seducing me!"

He recoiled as though physically struck. "Andy, that's not what happened."

Andrea watched him move around the room, feeling as though her heart weighed a ton. He wasn't happy about the baby, and why had she gotten maudlin over some old memories and decided he should know about his impending fatherhood? No, that hadn't been it. It had been that realization that she had never really stopped loving him. Oh, the flames had dimmed for a while, no question about it, but they'd always been lurking somewhere in her system.

He finally stopped pacing and looked at her. "I've never ever done anything right with you, have I?"

She could lie and agree with him, but she was through with lies and pretense. "Of course you have."

"In college?"

"Well...no...but..." She hesitated, but only for a second. This was something else that had to be said. "I always blamed you for our breakup in college. You were cruel."

Oddly the one thing she'd really wanted to say to him for weeks—for years, actually—didn't do a thing for her. It was all so long ago, and what did it signify now? She'd been much too unforgiving—a foolish, naive, unforgiving young girl. Even maturity hadn't softened her judgment, she had clung to the hurt for years, steadfastly believing that she had been wronged.

"I didn't mean to be," Keith said. "I thought you understood. That you wanted a business partnership just like I did. I guess I figured you'd know that eventually, when we became financially secure, which I was positive would happen, we'd get married."

"You never said that."

"I should have. I was so boiling over with ideas, plans and ambition. Regardless of all that, I did love you, Andy." He walked another circle around the room, then stopped directly in front of her, leaned over, put his hands on the arms of the chair and said, "I still do."

She swallowed. His face was close to hers and there was no avoiding his eyes. "I loved you, too," she said huskily. "Back then."

"But not now?"

She was afraid of giving too much too soon. "How can I know for sure what I feel? You weren't always so certain, either, or you wouldn't have hightailed it to Mexico to figure it out."

"Everything's different now. Andy, I want my baby."

"Which could be the reason you're talking about still loving me. Keith, it's not *your* baby until I say it is."

He frowned. "Wait a minute. Are you saying…?"

She broke in. "No! It's your baby, but that doesn't mean you can have it."

"What *does* it mean, then? If you intended to withhold our child from me, why did you tell me about it?"

"I got sentimental."

"And now you're sorry you did?"

"I don't know what I am!"

"Well, maybe you should figure it out!"

"Don't you dare yell at me!"

To preserve his own sanity and self-control, Keith walked away from her. Again he paced the room, thinking, remembering. They had more intertwined memories at thirty-eight than a lot of couples had at sixty. And he *did* love her, but she was so damn stubborn, and if she had it in her head that he'd only told her he loved her because of the baby, it would be almost impossible to change her mind.

He had to try, though. "Andy, how were you going to explain a baby without a husband?"

"There are lots of ways. Sperm banks, for one. Women don't need a man to have a baby these days, Keith."

"That's just great," he muttered darkly.

She felt awful. They should be rejoicing together, laughing, crying, making plans. Instead they were still fighting, still on different roads. Not even that, actually. Same road, different lanes was more like it, she thought sadly.

She thought of the baby then and laid her hand on her lower abdomen. It was so new, just beginning to form, but in her mind it was a fully developed infant. That was how she would always think of it till the day of its birth. Until that momentous day, she and nature would be its protectors, but then, didn't her precious son or daughter deserve to have both parents?

She could tell how hurt Keith was, and she could certainly feel her own pain. But she still loved him and it *was* possible that he hadn't said he loved her just to be part of his child's life.

She took a shaky breath. "Maybe…maybe we should try something."

Keith stopped and looked at her. "Try what?"

"To…to stop bickering and maybe…make it work…between us."

"Even though you don't love me?"

"Keith, that's not fair."

"But is it accurate?" He rushed over to her chair and knelt

at her knees. "Andy, you've denied my existence for eighteen years. Was I really that terrible in college?"

She was having trouble meeting his eyes. "No, but I
thought you were."

"You still thought it the night of the ball, didn't you?"

"I was afraid of you."

"Because I made you feel things you didn't want to feel?"

"Possibly." After a second she added, "Probably."

"Look at me." He put his hands on her face, one on each
side, and repeated softly, "Look at me, Andy." When she
finally did, he said, "I think you do love me. What do you
propose we do to try and make it work between us?"

She was losing her nerve again. "How about designing a
board indicating all possible choices and then throwing darts
at it?"

"I thought you were serious." He got up. "Maybe we
should sleep on it and talk again tomorrow."

It was Andrea's turn to panic. She got to her feet. "No,
don't go. I'm thinking that we might have been married to
each other for years and already have had children. Instead,
because of our fight and our own blindness, we went our
separate ways. We're going to have a baby. I already love
this child and you said you want it. Do you love it, too, or
do you merely want to preserve the Owens dynasty?" She
held up a hand to stop him from speaking. "Let me finish. I
think I do love you, and if you can honestly say that you
love me *and* the baby, then…"

Thunderstruck, Keith couldn't remain silent a moment
longer. "Then we should get married!" He pulled her into
his arms and began kissing her forehead, her cheeks and her
lips. None lingered in any one spot, and she closed her eyes
and savored the delicious sensation of his lips wandering and
exploring her face. For the first time since the ball she *felt*
loved.

"I truly adore you," he said huskily. "I mean it. I love
you, I love you, I love you. I always have. I love the baby,
and I swear to be the best father ever. I admit I ran off to

think. I admit loving you so much scared me, but that was mostly because I wasn't sure of your feelings. Even making love with me wasn't proof of love, sweetheart. So there it is. I love everything about you, every single thing, and now I want you to say it.''

"Are we playing another game?'' she whispered, for truly, his speech had stunned her.

"Not this time.''

She dampened her lips with her tongue and sucked in a breath. "All right, I'll say it. I adore you,'' she whispered as tears gathered in her eyes. "Keith, I'm so weary of all the pulling and pushing we did. I just want to be happy.''

"With me and our child.''

"Yes, with you and our child.''

He hugged her so tightly she laughed. "Keith, I can't breathe!''

Laughing, he loosened his hold on her and leaned his head back enough to look into her eyes. "You are so beautiful.''

"Keith, I'm not.''

"Fishing for more compliments, are we?'' he teased. "Let me start with…''

"No! Stop that now. We need to talk.''

"Fine. We could get married as soon as Texas law permits, if that's what you want, or we could fly to Las Vegas and do it tomorrow.''

"Let's be sensible about this and not rush the…the wedding. I'd really like to spend some quality time together, now that we're both out in the open with our feelings.''

"I guess that makes sense. All right, how about if we see each other every day and call each other at least three times a day. We should also go to every public place in town so everyone knows we are now a couple. I should meet your friends and you should meet mine. And we should make love at least once every day, no, make that twice a day. At *least* twice a day.''

Andrea was too breathlessly ecstatic to speak, for the dream she'd lived on in college was finally happening and it wasn't easy to believe. Had she hoped or even suspected Keith might go this far when she finally admitted—out loud and to his face—her love?

"And when we're ready...we'll know when the time is right...we'll get married," Keith continued. "Did I hit the right choice on the dart board?" he asked with an adorably enchanting grin.

"You did...yes."

Keith looked off across the room and after a few moments murmured, "It's still raining, coming down in buckets, it sounds like." Then he brought his gaze back to Andrea, who was by this time dangerously weak in the knees.

"Let's go to bed, sweetheart," he said, low and seductively.

"Yes," she whispered. She could say nothing else.

Thirteen

Three days remained of Kiddie Kingdom's spring term. On Monday, Andrea talked to Nancy Pringle, the principal, and asked if she could have a few more weeks to decide which term she wanted to take off this year. Her request surprised Nancy, and Andrea didn't explain that she couldn't go forward with either retirement or her normal summer-term break without a little more thought. Teaching had always meant so much to her, and she was finding it hard to imagine life without it. After all, she taught at a liberal preschool that permitted teacher-moms to bring their babies—and, of course, their toddlers—to class. If she wanted to continue teaching she would really only need to take off a month or so after the baby's birth. She hadn't yet discussed it with Keith, but she would.

Nancy said yes to her request, which pleased Andrea, but for a fact, nearly everything, even a simple ''Good morning'' from a stranger, pleased her now. Her mood was remarkably upbeat, there seemed to be a permanent smile on her face, and just thinking of Keith warmed her.

In truth she had never known the power and magic of the kind of love she felt from and for Keith. Her self-confidence soared because of it; her energy level rose because of it; the sky was bluer because of it. She was so glad and thrilled to be alive and in love, so thankful, and in gratitude for this miracle of fate or gift from above she would not let herself lament past mistakes and misjudgments, not her own, not Keith's.

They spent every possible moment together. When she got home from school on Monday he was waiting for her. That afternoon he invited her to *his* house, and indeed it was a mansion, enormous, overly decorated and not at all the kind of home she admired. But she walked through the rooms with him and in one of the bedrooms—not the master suite, she noted—they made such sweet and tender love that she wept.

Then they talked. "When we're married, where would you like to live?" Keith asked.

"Well…" She didn't want to say that she didn't like his mansion, because he must like it or he wouldn't be living in it.

"I opt for your house or a new one that we would plan and build together," he said.

His sweet unselfishness moved her, and she kissed him with all the love in her heart. Later they discussed her teaching career, and he told her to do whatever she wanted. "You know you'll never have to work a day of your life, but I know you love teaching, and now I even know why you do. It's up to you, sweetheart."

She thought that was sweet, as well.

They ate out that night, choosing Claire's, Royal's fine French restaurant. They saw people they knew and people they knew saw them. They smiled at each other because people would know they were a couple. It was what they wanted.

On Tuesday they went to Claire's with some of the Cattleman's Club members for dinner. Despite Andrea's increased self-confidence, she felt a bit nervous about that. But Keith's friends seemed genuinely pleased to meet her—she'd met some of them at the charity ball, though she hadn't even tried to remember names and faces at the time—and the evening turned out to be great fun.

Wednesday was the last day of the spring term, and Andrea brought cookies to school as a special treat for her tiny students. She also invited Keith to the party, and when he arrived she asked him to read the "cluck-cluck" story to the class.

This time while he read she could not keep tears at bay. She was looking at such a beautiful, touching scene, her beloved reading aloud to ten adorable children, and it made her think of the tiny life she was carrying. Keith talked often of the baby—asking dozens of questions about how she felt and could she feel it inside her yet—and she now believed with all her heart that he was as elated with their impending parenthood as she was.

That night Andrea entertained her friends and introduced Keith to them. She saw a few surprised faces in the group, but all in all the evening went well and Keith was accepted. After everyone had gone home, he hugged Andrea and laughingly said, "I think I passed muster."

"Indeed you did, darling," she agreed and snuggled closer to him.

Thursday was their first completely free day, and they decided to take a long, lazy drive and just enjoy themselves *by* themselves. It was a fabulous day, full of kisses, teasing and laughter with some reminiscing thrown in—How could they not talk about their conjoined childhood on occasion?—and they got back to Royal a little before eight that evening, ecstatically happy, a little tired and very hungry.

"Let's stop at the diner for one of Manny's burgers," Keith suggested.

"And a slice of his coconut-cream pie," Andrea agreed. "Oh, that sounds perfect. I'm famished."

And so they went to the diner. Because of the hour only

a few other people were there, and, to their surprise, the customers were all strangers, no one either of them knew.

Keith led the way to one of the back booths, then excused himself and went to the men's room. Two glasses of water in plastic glasses were placed on the table, along with two menus. Andrea glanced up and saw Laura Edwards. Laura looked, Andrea realized with a sad and sinking sensation, even more haggard than the last time she'd seen her.

"Hello, Laura," she said quietly.

"Andrea," Laura acknowledged while looking around, as though expecting someone to pounce on her from behind. Andrea experienced a chill, for she was positive now that Laura was desperately afraid of someone. "Is it still all right if I call you at home?" the waitress whispered. "I'm off tomorrow and I think I could find a way to call without...without..." Her voice broke, convincing Andrea even more of her terror. But then she managed to add, "Maybe we could meet somewhere."

"Of course we could. I'll meet you anywhere you wish."

Keith returned and Laura scurried away. He smiled at Andrea and asked, "Did you order for us?"

Andrea leaned forward. "Laura and I were talking. Keith, she's scared to death of someone and she's going to call me tomorrow to set up a meeting. I think she's reached the point of having to talk about it and I..."

Keith was so stunned he couldn't immediately speak. Laura Edwards was the key person providing Dorian's alibi for the night of Eric Chamber's murder. They hadn't been able to disprove Dorian's claim, not when Laura claimed he was at the Royal Diner most of the night. Laura had stuck to her story. Did he want Andrea involved with this woman?

"Andrea, I don't want you getting hurt over someone else's troubles," he said, forcing calmness in his voice and sounding as though his stomach wasn't doing flips.

Andrea was startled. His objection was a complete surprise and puzzling. "Keith, I've helped quite a few women get through some very bad times and I've never once been in danger. Laura is in trouble and if I can help, I have to. That's what New Hope is all about. You wouldn't believe how many women are in abusive relationships, and I strongly suspect that's Laura's problem. Every time I see her she looks worse. Please understand.''

It wasn't a matter of understanding. He nearly broke his vow of silence about the club's covert activities and told her what he and the other members were working on right now. He was so concerned about her and the baby that he even opened his mouth to fill her in on the real facts of Laura Edward's desperation, even if they weren't completely clear in Keith's mind. But it made sense to him that Dorian might be a threatening force in her life now simply because she knew too much. Actually, if Andrea weren't involved—or *trying* to get involved—Keith would be elated about stumbling across Laura's present state of mind. But it was impossible for him to be elated over anything with Andrea crossing a line she didn't even know existed.

''Andy, tell her to go to New Hope. Isn't that what they do, take in women who are in trouble?''

Andrea frowned slightly. ''That's exactly what New Hope does, thanks to the generosity of people like you and your club friends, but it takes some abused women a very long time to reach the point of public acknowledgment of something that's been going on privately, possibly for years. Keith, darling, I have to do it her way. I *have* to. I'm going to wait for her call tomorrow. I'm sorry you disapprove but I know what I must do.''

Her determined expression wilted Keith's protests. He couldn't demand she stay away from Laura without a lengthy explanation he couldn't provide. He would watch over her and their baby in another way.

Internally shaken, he reached across the table and took her hand. ''I don't disapprove. Just be careful, okay?''

He only wanted to protect her from any possible harm, the darling man. She loved him so much at that moment that she had to blink back tears. ''I promise.''

* * *

The following morning, Keith told Andrea that he really should spend some time at his office—a lie—but he would call her around noon. He also asked—nicely—if she would call him when Laura Edwards phoned her, just so he would know where they were meeting. Holding her in his arms he said emotionally, "Maybe I shouldn't worry about you and the baby, but I do. Take care, sweetheart." He kissed her goodbye and left.

Andrea closed and locked the door behind him, then watched him drive away in his SUV through a side window. He'd stayed all night. Everyone in Royal had to know by now that Andrea O'Rourke and Keith Owens were lovers. Some of them were undoubtedly speculating about the duration of the romantic affair and if it would lead to marriage. Given her loner status for so long, Andrea couldn't fault normal curiosity.

Since she couldn't just sit around and wait for the phone to ring she sorted clothes and organized closets, and all the while, events since the ball passed through her mind. Her and Keith together again—and, perhaps, at long last— seemed like a fantasy. But it wasn't a fantasy, she reminded herself with a serene smile, it was real. Very real and very wonderful.

She was organizing her shoes when the phone rang. A glance at her watch as she went to answer told her it was noon. Time had really gotten away from her.

She picked up the phone. "Hello?"

It was Keith. "Hello, sweetheart. Any word from Laura?"

"Not yet. I hope something didn't happen to change her mind."

He hoped exactly the opposite, but he didn't say so. "You sound worried. Please don't let this get you down."

"I'll try. Are you still at your office?"

"No, I'm at the club." He'd been at the club all morning, along with Will, Rob, Sebastian and Jason. They'd broken Eric's numeric code; it was merely a record of his gambling wins and losses, with dates and sums. His losses had far exceeded his wins, and the dates coincided with money taken from Wescott Oil bank accounts. They had deduced the rest of the story. Dorian had discovered Eric's embezzlement and then blackmailed him into churning the accounting records to make Sebastian responsible, using more money to open an account in his name. Apparently Eric had done something to enrage Dorian and Dorian had killed him.

Problem was, they still had no proof of Dorian's guilt, mostly because of the airtight alibi provided by Laura Edwards. When Keith told them about Laura's plan to call Andrea for a meeting, their hopes had gone sky-high; maybe Laura was ready to turn the tables on that lie. They had literally sat on the edges of their seats, same as Keith had, all morning, waiting to hear from Andrea.

"It's business, too, sweetheart," Keith told Andrea, "a lunch meeting." He didn't like deceiving her like this, but he had to do what they all thought was right. Dorian was a dangerous individual, and now they were very close to acquiring the proof needed to send him to prison. At least it appeared that way. Keith swallowed but concealed the nervous tension in his gut. He was, after all, permitting the woman he loved to put herself at risk by even talking to Laura, even though he and the others in the group were prepared to protect Andrea at any cost. "The fastest way to reach me is by cell phone, Andy," he said quietly. "You know the number."

"Yes, I do. I also have the club's number."

"Andy, the second Laura calls, you call me. Promise?"

"Yes, dear, I promise," she replied teasingly. His concern was touching, if a bit silly. Well, maybe not silly, she amended. Some spouses and boyfriends were truly dangerous men, and if Laura was trying to escape a really horrible relationship, there was always the chance her brutal companion might blame anyone attempting to assist her.

But it had never happened to her with any other woman

seeking help, and Andrea couldn't get too worried that it might with Laura. She put it out of her mind.

It was three-thirty when the phone finally rang again. A bundle of nerves by then, Andrea raced for the instrument as though it were a direct line to life itself. "Hello?" she said anxiously.

"Andrea...this is Laura...you know, from the diner?"

"Yes...yes...I've been expecting your call. Laura, are you all right?"

"Yes, I'm fine. I...just couldn't get away until now. Andrea, I really can't talk on the phone."

Andrea drew a calming breath, but she still felt rattled. "We'll talk face to face. Where would you like to meet? Do you have a particular place in mind?"

"No...I...just don't know," Laura stammered. "Do you know someplace, uh, safe?"

Andrea was beginning to think more clearly. Laura might still be in danger but she hadn't yet been harmed. She, Andrea, had to keep them both on the right track.

"Yes, I do," she said firmly. "Where are you now?"

"At the pay phone on the corner of Jennings and Fifth. Do you know where that is?"

"Yes. Laura, let me pick you up and bring you to my house."

"Your house? I was afraid you were going to say New Hope. I can't go there, Andrea. Too many people would see me."

"No one will see you at my home. Laura, are you afraid that someone's watching you now?"

"It's...possible," Laura whispered. "Maybe it's my imagination. I...really don't know."

Laura's fear gave Andrea a shiver. She'd never experienced that kind of fear herself, but she'd seen it in women's eyes. Hearing it in Laura's voice increased Andrea's determination to help.

"All right, here's what we'll do," she said into the phone. "Hang up and go into that little bookstore near the corner. I think it's the second shop from the corner. Act as though you're browsing the shelves but keep an eye on the street. My car is a dark-blue sedan. I'll double-park directly in front of the bookstore and wait for you. It shouldn't take more than ten minutes to get there, but wait twenty minutes just in case some unforeseen traffic problem slows me down.''

"All right. Bye…and thanks.''

"I'll see you shortly.'' Andrea hung up, then dialed Keith's cell phone. She didn't know if he was still at the club—it seemed a long time for him to have been there, even for a business meeting—but with his cell phone he was reachable anywhere in Royal.

"Andrea?'' he said by way of greeting after one ring. "Did she call?''

"Yes.'' Andrea explained that she was picking Laura up at Jennings and Fifth and bringing her back to the house.

"Good. But if anything at all happens that you don't expect, call me at once.''

"Keith, is something wrong? Nothing unexpected is going to happen. Well, I suppose the person she's afraid of could…''

"Andrea, listen to me. Don't let anyone but Laura get in your car. Keep the back doors locked and once you have Laura, drive directly home.''

"You big worrywart,'' she said adoringly. "I'll be fine.''

"And call me the minute you get home.''

"Yes, dear. I have to run. Laura will be standing around worrying. Love you. Bye.'' She hung up, gathered her purse and car keys from where she'd placed them in anticipation of Laura's call and then hurried to the garage. Jennings and Fifth was in downtown Royal, which seemed busier than normal to Andrea, and it took almost fifteen minutes for her to get there. She double-parked in front of the bookstore, Laura bounded outside and jumped into the car and Andrea immediately drove away.

Oddly, Andrea felt a strong sense of relief. Her tension had probably been caused by Keith's long list of cautions, she decided, but could she fault him for loving her so much? And he was thinking of the baby, too, of course.

"This is so good of you," Laura said while dabbing at her eyes with a wad of tissues. "I…I guess I've been wondering why a woman like you would put herself at risk to help someone like me."

At risk? A chill traveled Andrea's spine. "Am I in danger, Laura?"

"Well…I guess you could be…if he saw me get in your car…I guess." She sounded miserable, very apologetic and she said again, "I can't believe a woman like you would go out of her way to help someone like me."

Andrea began checking the rearview mirror, although she suspected she wouldn't know if they were being followed unless someone hooked his front bumper onto her back bumper. She wasn't a detective, after all. Unquestionably she was vastly more concerned now than she'd been, but she was also committed and had to see this through.

"We're not as different from each other as you might think, Laura," she said, striving for her normal composure in dealing with an abused woman.

"You're wrong," Laura said listlessly. "I know in my soul that you could never do what I did."

Andrea sent her passenger a sharp look. "What *you* did?"

"I…I have to tell someone about it," Laura whispered hoarsely. "I can't live with it any longer."

Andrea's alert alarm went off the scale. She'd been so certain that Laura's problem was an abusive partner, and now Laura was talking about something *she* had done.

Andrea's grip on the steering wheel tightened and her stomach tensed. She could be in over her head with Laura, but she couldn't just put her off now, could she? The woman was in trouble, trapped in a torment of emotional agony, and she was seeking relief. No, Andrea thought, she couldn't turn her back on Laura, whatever her story.

She couldn't help being on edge, though, and she kept driving with one eye on the rearview mirror, just in case she *was* able to spot someone following them. She saw nothing out of the ordinary, just what appeared to her eyes as Royal's usual traffic, but a clever driver could outwit an amateur like her any day of the week. It was incredibly relieving to finally drive through the gates of Pine Valley and ultimately turn onto her street. A look in the rearview mirror was reassuring; not one other car was in sight.

At her house Andrea parked in the garage and immediately lowered the door. The two women went inside and in the kitchen Andrea asked, "Do you like herbal tea, Laura?" As jumpy as Laura was, Andrea didn't think feeding her caffeine was a good idea.

"Uh, sure…yes…thanks," Laura mumbled.

"Don't be nervous. You're perfectly safe here. Sit at the table. It won't take a minute to prepare the tea." Andrea put the teakettle on the stove and said, "I have to make a phone call, Laura. I'll only be a minute." She hurried to the den and dialed Keith's cell phone.

"She's here," she said at once. "Keith, she hinted at something *she* did. I think I was wrong about her being trapped in an abusive relationship."

Keith clenched his free fist. He was positive now about what Laura was going to tell Andrea, and while he gave a nod to his friends, no one smiled. This was serious business for all of them.

But he couldn't stop himself from cautioning her again. "Andy, I'm going to have this phone in my hand until I hear from you again. If even one tiny thing occurs that seems out of sync, you are to call me immediately."

This time Andrea wasn't flippant. Something was wrong. She had no idea what it might be, but she sensed that it was crucial that she do exactly as Keith asked. "I will, darling." She hung up and hurried back to the kitchen.

"Your house is nice," Laura said shyly when Andrea walked in.

"Thank you. I like it."

"I live in an apartment. It's…pretty nice."

"Which apartment complex, Laura?"

"The Caplan Arms."

"Oh, yes, I know the place. There's the teakettle." Andrea quickly prepared the tea and brought it to the table. She sat across from Laura and smiled, though she realized that she honestly did not feel like smiling. In fact there seemed to be a sizable knot of nerves in her stomach. "Now we can talk. A cup of tea always relaxes me."

Laura managed a wan smile. "Tea is nice."

And then Andrea sipped tea and forced herself to wait quietly for Laura to begin the conversation. Finally Laura asked, "Do you know about the investigation of the murder of Eric Chambers?"

Andrea was so stunned—she never could have imagined *that* subject coming out of Laura's mouth—that she lowered her cup and actually gaped wide-eyed at the woman. Laura hadn't committed murder, had she?

"Not entirely," she managed to say, albeit rather weakly. "Why?"

"I…I think…no, I'm certain…of who the murderer is."

Andrea could feel the color drain from her face. "How…how would you know that?"

"I provided the killer's alibi," Laura whispered. "Actually, I *am* the killer's alibi. Oh, Andrea, it's all so awful." She started crying and Andrea rushed—albeit on shaky legs—to get her some fresh tissues. Her heart was pounding so furiously that her hands were trembling when she placed a box of tissues on the table next to Laura's cup. "Thank you," Laura managed to gasp between great heaving sobs.

Returning to her chair, Andrea wondered frantically what she should do. Did she want to hear Laura's story now? Laura was talking about murder, the murder of that poor man who had worked at Wescott Oil. She should be talking to the police, not to a New Hope volunteer!

But dare she say something of that nature to Laura? The woman felt safe in talking to her. She couldn't destroy that trust and tell Laura to take her story to the police. She would listen and then decide how to deal with this shocking turn. She would call Keith, of course, but first she would listen.

Laura eventually calmed down, got control of her emotions and began speaking. ''I had a crush on Sebastian Wescott for years and years. He never knew I was alive, but I still fantasized about him. I know it was silly, but I couldn't help myself.'' Laura sighed. ''Then about six months ago his half brother, Dorian Brady, came to Royal. Do you know Sebastian and Dorian?''

''I've met them, yes.'' Dorian Brady? That man who had insisted on an introduction at the ball? ''Please go on.''

''Dorian's very handsome with his chestnut brown hair and silver-gray eyes. He began paying attention to me, and I was flattered. I mean, he looked so much like Sebastian and I…I guess I was a fool for falling for his line…but he was so charming and I was so lonely and frustrated over Sebastian never noticing me. I began seeing Dorian. For a while it was nice between us, but then one night he told me that he was going to come into the diner quite late. He asked me to seat him in a back booth, bring him some food and then go about my business. He…he slipped out the back door, unnoticed by anyone else in the place, and…and I think he must have killed Mr. Chambers. He made me swear to tell anyone who asked that he'd never left the diner, and I've done that, Andrea. I've lied to the police and to Sebastian's friends who keep asking me.''

Andrea whispered, ''Are you sure he did it?''

''I'm pretty sure. He's got a terrible temper. He's a dangerous man, and…and I'm scared to death of him.''

Andrea was so unnerved she could barely think. But one question suddenly formed clear as glass in her stunned brain. ''Sebastian's friends?'' she repeated slowly, and then added, ''Who are?''

''Members of the Cattleman's Club. It's a very close-knit society. They made Dorian a member, so I can't say anything to them, because then he'd know!''

Keith was involved in that investigation, she knew it now.

It was the reason he'd been so concerned about her having anything to do with Laura.

It hurt to learn there were facets to Keith she knew nothing about; she'd been so positive of knowing Keith through and through now. But this secret involvement, this secret society wearing the face of an ordinary club for men…he could have told her about it, couldn't he? Didn't he trust her?

"Why…why would Dorian kill Eric?" Andrea asked in a choked voice. "Did he tell you that?"

"He's rambled on about it several times, but I kind of pieced it together for myself. Mr. Chambers was an accountant at Wescott Oil. Dorian said he had Mr. Chambers in his back pocket. I think Dorian talked him into accessing some computer accounts and moving money around to make it look like Sebastian was stealing from the company. I know Dorian was trying to get Sebastian in trouble. He's told me often enough how he resents Sebastian because *he* was never acknowledged by their father and Sebastian was the apple of Jack Wescott's eye. I think Eric Chambers threatened to go to Sebastian because Dorian was furious with him."

"I see," Andrea murmured, and then made a decision. "Laura, I hate saying this but you might be in terrible danger. If Dorian killed Eric then he could be planning the same fate for you."

"I know. I've been half-crazy ever since it happened." Laura's eyes filled again. "Andrea, I didn't know Dorian was planning murder that night. I thought he was merely going to do something to get back at Sebastian."

"And you couldn't help resenting Sebastian because he never noticed you as a woman."

"It was so stupid."

"Well, we're not always sensible and smart, are we? Laura, do you want my advice?"

"Yes. I…I'm afraid to go to the police on my own."

"You need a good lawyer. I'm going to call one and set up a meeting for you."

Laura looked downcast, but she nodded. "All right."

Andrea left the kitchen and hurried to the den, where she looked up a telephone number and dialed it. In minutes she had permission to bring Laura to the lawyer's office immediately. She put down the phone without calling Keith.

Returning to the kitchen, she picked up her purse from the counter and said, "Let's go, Laura. You need to get this awful mess straightened out, once and for all."

Laura got to her feet. "Do you think I'll have to go to jail?"

"I don't know. I hope not, but I simply do not know. Do you still want to see that lawyer?"

Laura nodded. "I have to do something. I can't live like this anymore. Let's go."

Andrea was back home in thirty minutes. She'd left Laura in capable, sympathetic hands, and now she knew she should talk to Keith and let him know that she didn't like being deliberately left out of what appeared to be an important part of his life. Yes, he was a businessman, but he was also a...a what? A private investigator, a soldier of fortune, damn it, what?

She paced and stewed and shed a few tears and asked herself how she could ever trust him again. And she'd just *learned* to trust him! Did he love her or didn't he? After this it was very easy to think that his "in love" behavior was an act to gain possession of his child.

She *had* to call him. There was too much bottled up inside her to go on like this. She punched out his cell number and he answered on the first ring again.

"Are you okay?" he asked right out of the starting gate.

She got right to the heart of it. "Keith, are you involved in the investigation of Eric Chamber's murder?"

Keith's heart sank. "Andy, where are you?"

"Home. Alone." She quickly and in a razor-sharp voice related what had taken place with Laura. "I'm not very happy right now, Keith. You've been lying to me."

"No, honey, no! I never lied, I just omitted some things because of a vow of silence."

"A vow of silence! What in hell is that club, a branch of the CIA?"

"I swear I was going to tell you everything after we were married."

"Meaning I'm not trustworthy now?"

"Andy, please don't take it like that. I was just trying to do what was best for all concerned."

"Well, I don't mind admitting that I'm a little disappointed in you, Keith. Oh, my God, what's that noise?"

"Andrea, I hear it. What is it?"

"I think…it sounded like shattering glass! Keith, I think someone's in the house! I didn't set the alarm when I got home!"

"Get out of the house, now! I'm on my way!" The phone went dead. Andrea had hung up, or someone had hung up for her. "Someone's in Andrea's house! It's probably Dorian!" he yelled as he slammed down the phone.

Everyone jumped up and followed him outside, where they piled into cars and left the club's parking lot with their tires squealing. Keith drove with a murderous rage pumping adrenaline through his system. Somehow he'd gotten ahead of the pack in his SUV, though they weren't far behind him. But he increased the distance by skidding around corners and driving like a maniac, swearing he would kill Dorian if he had harmed Andrea.

Andrea found herself looking down the barrel of a gun. It was in the right hand of Dorian Brady. He'd been on Laura's trail all day, and he'd figured out that she'd told Andrea everything. Well, if he thought she was going to weep and whimper, he had another thought coming.

"You can't kill the whole town, Dorian," she said in the steadiest voice she could manage. "Laura is talking to a lawyer right now, and then he will talk to the police and it will go on and on, ad infinitum. Your goose is cooked, face it."

"You meddling busybody," he hissed. "Forever passing out cards with your phone number so women who deserve exactly what they're getting from men can call you and lap up your sickeningly sweet sympathy."

"Oh, you're going straight to the penitentiary, mister, and that's what *you* deserve!"

"Not before I make sure you never ruin another man's life, you bitch!" Dorian straightened his right arm and took aim, and Andrea shut her eyes, for she could already feel the red-hot bullet ripping through her flesh.

Only, instead of a gunshot, she heard a loud thud and a yelp. Her eyes flew open; Keith had Dorian down on the floor and was using him for a punching bag. The gun had slid under a chair.

Andrea was afraid that Keith was going to kill Dorian, the way he was punching him. "No, Keith, don't! Stop, you're going too far!"

"He was going to shoot you!" Keith said through furiously clenched teeth.

"But he didn't, and I don't want you killing him! Please, just stop."

Keith's head dropped forward for a moment, then he climbed off Dorian and staggered to his feet. He put his arms around Andrea. "Thank God I got here in time."

Dorian was bloodied and beaten, and he knew what was in store for him. Moving cautiously and slowly he scooted over until he could reach his gun under the chair.

Then he stumbled to his feet, with the gun. "Stay where you are or I'll kill you both."

Andrea could feel Keith stiffen. "I knew I should have knocked you cold," he said angrily.

"I'm not going to jail for this. Don't do anything stupid and force me to shoot you." Dorian darted from the room just seconds before the arrival of the rest of the Cattleman's Club posse.

"It's Dorian, just as we suspected. He went out the back way," Keith announced, and all of them ran through the house. Just as they reached the door with the shattered glass window, they heard a gunshot.

Stunned, they peered outside and saw Dorian on the ground near the pool. "He shot himself," Keith announced. "I'm sorry, Sebastian."

"It's probably best, Keith," Sebastian said soberly. "Sad and unnecessary, but best, considering his criminal behavior."

They trooped over to the body, made sure Dorian didn't still have a pulse and then returned to the house. Keith phoned for the police.

The rest of the day was a nightmare. A number of police cars, an ambulance, the coroner's vehicle and even a fire truck had answered Keith's 911 call.

"There goes the neighborhood," Keith said dryly when everyone had finally departed.

Andrea tried to smile, but it simply wasn't in her. However evil Dorian Brady had been, he'd still been a human being and he'd killed himself in *her* backyard. She would not easily get over today's devastating events, she knew.

Keith made sure the doors were locked and the security system armed for Andrea's benefit. She truly looked as though she couldn't take one more scare, not even a small one. Then he returned to the living room, sat next to her on the sofa and pulled her into his arms.

"Try to relax and forget," he murmured, his lips in her hair. "It's over and done with."

She snuggled closer to him. "I feel safe with you."

"Good. Andy…" He held her all during his explanation of the Cattleman's Club involvement in secret missions to save innocent people's lives. "But you have to understand that what we do is not for publication, sweetheart."

"I'm sorry I got all upset when Laura told me about the club. Dorian must have told her. Anyhow, I won't breathe a word of it, but is that, uh, practice going to continue? I mean, anytime you're not at home should I worry that you might be off on some dangerous mission?"

Keith laughed. "Of course not." What other answer could he give her? *Yes, my love, it's entirely possible that when I'm off on some supposed business trip, I'm really up to my eyeballs in a covert mission.* No, he couldn't lay that on her now, not after all she'd gone through today. And he would never, ever do or say anything that might endanger the safety of the baby in her body.

"Then I can count on you to let me know if another...if another Dorian enters the picture, and you're involved and you might be in danger?"

"You were the one in danger today, Andy," he said gently. "Not me. Are you going to continue your work for New Hope?"

"I'd...like to."

"I feel exactly the same about what I've been doing."

They hugged each other tightly for a long time. They were both committed to helping less fortunate people than themselves, and neither could ask the other to stop.

"How much time do you need to plan a wedding?" Keith asked softly.

Andrea's pulse quickened. "A formal wedding or a simple affair?"

"Which do you prefer?"

"Simple." Her face was against his chest and she could hear the beating of his heart.

"Then let's do it as soon as the big day can be arranged."

"Oh, Keith!" She adjusted her position on the sofa so she could throw her arms around his neck. "I love you so much!"

"Honey, uh, I just have one request. I'd like to hold a reception...after the ceremony, of course...at the club. Can you deal with that?"

"If you can deal with my friends, I can deal with yours."

"Then we have no problem." Keith's eyes were suddenly misty. "Oh, Andy, we should have always been together. Why did I let you get away in college?"

"Far more important than that question is what made you

start chasing me again after so many years. I think it was because we hadn't slept together before. I was the one that got away and you couldn't stand it."

"But you didn't *really* get away, did you? It just took me a lot longer to nail you than it should have."

Andrea slugged him a good one on his arm. "You toad!"

Keith grinned. "Come here, sweetheart, and show me how much you love me."

Sighing happily, she did exactly that.

Two weeks later the local newspaper reported the wedding. Along with photographs of the bride and groom, there was an article. It read:

Keith Owens, sole owner and operator of Owens Techware Company, and Andrea O'Rourke, nursery-school teacher and volunteer for numerous charities, were married in a private ceremony yesterday. A reception was held at the Texas Cattleman's Club immediately after, and it was indeed a splendid event.

The new Mrs. Owens was radiant in a white on white, ankle-length gown and Mr. Owens wore a pale gray Western-cut suit. An extremely handsome couple, they greeted hundreds of guests as they arrived at the club with a gift of a wrist corsage of white orchids for the ladies and an orchid boutonniere for the gentlemen.

Dinner was served buffet-style and consisted of baron of beef, barbecued ribs, turkey, ham, delightful and delicious salads and side dishes, and last but far from least a number of Mexican favorites, such as enchiladas and tamales. An excellent champagne was served throughout the reception.

Some of the guests, to name a few, were Sterling and Susan Churchill, Blake and Joselyn Hunt, Aaron and Pamela Black, Dakota and Kathy Lewis, William and Diana Bradford and Sebastian and Susan Wescott. All in all it was a grand affair and it appeared that everyone had a marvelous time.

Before saying good-night to everyone, the groom announced that he was whisking his bride to the Bahamas for a romantic honeymoon, after which he said they would return to Royal to plan the construction of their new home.

Congratulations and best wishes to Royal's newest married couple, Keith and Andrea Owens!

* * * * *

presents

A brand-new miniseries about the Connellys of Chicago,
a wealthy, powerful American family tied by blood to the
royal family of the island kingdom of Altaria.
They're wealthy, powerful and rocked by
scandal, betrayal…and passion!

Look for a whole year of glamorous and
utterly romantic tales in 2002:

Where love comes alive™

Continues the captivating series from
bestselling author
BARBARA McCAULEY

SECRETS!

Hidden legacies, hidden loves—revel in the
unfolding of the Blackhawk siblings' deepest, most
desirable SECRETS!

Don't miss the next irresistible books in the series...

TAMING BLACKHAWK
On Sale May 2002
(SD #1437)

IN BLACKHAWK'S BED
On Sale July 2002
(SD #1447)

And look for another title on sale in 2003!

Available at your favorite retail outlet.

Where love comes alive™

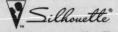

COMING NEXT MONTH

#1447 IN BLACKHAWK'S BED—Barbara McCauley
Man of the Month/Secrets!
Experience had taught loner Seth Blackhawk not to believe in
happily-ever-after. Then one day he saved the life of a little girl.
Hannah Michaels, the child's mother, sent desire surging through
him. But did he have the courage to accept the love she offered?

#1448 THE ROYAL & THE RUNAWAY BRIDE—
Kathryn Jensen
Dynasties: The Connellys
Vowing not to be used for her money again, Alexandra Connelly ran
away to Altaria and posed as a horse trainer. There she met sexy
Prince Phillip Kinrowan, whose intoxicating kisses made her dizzy
with desire. The irresistible prince captured her heart, and she longed
for the right moment to tell him the truth about herself.

#1449 COWBOY'S SPECIAL WOMAN—Sara Orwig
Nothing had prepared wanderer Jake Reiner for the sizzling attraction
between him and Maggie Langford. Her beauty and warmth tempted
him, and soon he yearned to claim her. Somehow he had to convince
her that he wanted her—not just for today, but for eternity!

#1450 THE SECRET MILLIONAIRE—Ryanne Corey
Wealthy cop Zack Daniels couldn't believe his luck when he found
himself locked in a basement with leggy blonde Anna Smith. Things
only got better as she offered him an undercover assignment…as her
boyfriend-of-convenience. Make-believe romance soon turned to real
passion, but what would happen once his temporary assignment ended?

#1451 CINDERELLA & THE PLAYBOY—Laura Wright
Abby McGrady was stunned when millionaire CEO C. K. Tanner
asked her to be his pretend wife so he could secure a business deal.
But after unexpected passion exploded between them, Abby found
herself falling for devastatingly handsome Tanner. She wanted to make
their temporary arrangement permanent. Now she just had to convince
her stubborn bachelor he wanted the same thing.

#1452 ZANE: THE WILD ONE—Bronwyn Jameson
A good man was proving hard to find for Julia Goodwin. Then former
bad boy Zane Lucas came back to town. Their attraction boiled over
when circumstances threw them together, and they spent one long, hot
night together. But Julia wanted forever, and dangerous, sexy-as-sin
Zane wasn't marriage material…or was he?

SDCNM0602